CLAIM TO
FAME

ALSO BY MARGARET PETERSON HADDIX

CLAIM TO FAME

MARGARET PETERSON HADDIX

SIMON & SCHUSTER BFYR

NEW YORK   LONDON   TORONTO   SYDNEY

SIMON & SCHUSTER BFYR

An imprint of Simon & Schuster Children's Publishing Division
1230 Avenue of the Americas, New York, New York 10020

For information about special discounts for bulk purchases, please contact Simon & Schuster
Special Sales at 1-866-506-1949 or business@simonandschuster.com.
The Simon & Schuster Speakers Bureau can bring authors to your live event. For more
information or to book an event, contact the Simon & Schuster Speakers Bureau at
1-866-248-3049 or visit our website at www.simonspeakers.com.
Also available in a SIMON & SCHUSTER BFYR hardcover edition.
Book design by Laurent Linn
The text for this book is set in ITC Giovanni Standard.
Manufactured in the United States of America
First SIMON & SCHUSTER BFYR paperback edition November 2010
4 6 8 10 9 7 5
The Library of Congress has cataloged the hardcover edition as follows:
Haddix, Margaret Peterson.
Claim to fame / Margaret Peterson Haddix.—1st ed.
p. cm.
Summary: Sixteen-year-old Lindsay, a former child star whose career ended when she
developed the ability to hear what anyone, anywhere says about her and apparently suffered
a nervous breakdown, comes to see this as an asset when, after her father's death, she learns
that she is not alone.
ISBN 978-1-4169-3917-7 (hc)
[1. Extrasensory Perception—Fiction. 2. Fame—Fiction. 3. Actors and Actresses—Fiction.
4. Grief—Fiction. 5. Emotional Problems—Fiction. 6. Illinois—Fiction.] 1. Title.
PZ7.H1164 Clc 2009
[Fic]—dc22
2008040792
ISBN 978-1-4169-3918-4 (pbk)
ISBN 978-1-4169-9737-5 (eBook)
1013 MTN

For Kathy

CLAIM TO FAME

Chapter 1

I was supposed to be doing my algebra homework that night. Nobody ever tells you, "Do your algebra and it will keep you safe. It will protect you from being kidnapped."

Nobody ever says that. But in my case, that night, it might have been true.

I didn't do my algebra homework. I should have—I'd made a promise to my dad, after all. But it was such a soft spring night, the first evening since October that had had any warmth to it. It was one of those nights when you can almost feel the seasons changing, when you can begin to hope that you're done with bitter cold and dead earth and harsh winter winds. It'd just be *wrong* to use a night like that for algebra homework.

So instead of picking up my pencil and solving for x, I climbed out my bedroom window and sat on my balcony, my arms wrapped around my legs, my back against the wall, my chin perched on my knees.

When I say "balcony," you're probably picturing something out of *Romeo and Juliet,* maybe with lacy wrought-iron fleur-de-lis on the railing, a place where I could lean out and sigh longingly as my boyfriend called up to me from below. In reality I didn't have a boyfriend, and it was actually a bit of a stretch to say that I had a balcony. My house—ours, I mean, where I lived with my father—was a rickety one-and-a-half-story wood-framed box. Springdale's a college town, and the houses here were built for penny-pinching college students and only-slightly-less-impoverished professors whose minds would be so filled with deep thoughts that they might not notice cracks in the foundation and walls that met at skewed angles. So my "balcony" was just a flat section of roof, unevenly shingled, with a wobbly wood railing barely more than ankle high, and an equally wobbly wooden staircase trailing down the side of the house to the ground. My father used to theorize that the staircase dated back to the early 1900s, when our house was a rooming house for college girls, and the housemother might have been too deaf to hear the girls sneaking out at night.

I'm pretty sure that's not the kind of musing an ordinary father would share with his daughter. Fathers generally don't tell daughters about ways to escape. But the way I'd lived for the past five years, even my absentminded father must have seen that it would take much more than a rickety staircase to draw me away.

So there I was on the balcony, staring out at the beginnings of buds on the limbs of our maple tree. Occasionally clusters of college students would pass by on the sidewalk down below, coming back from the library or the bars or meetings where they were planning to save the endangered American burying beetle or planning to aid the refugees of some war nobody else had ever even heard of. (Springdale College was founded by reformers attempting to bring their utopian ideals to the Midwest—its students had a long tradition of working for obscure lost causes.) I wasn't really listening to the bursts of excited chatter drifting up to me through the maple boughs; I wasn't really thinking about how deceptive it was that those college students seemed so nearby when really we were living in completely different worlds. They would have heard me, easily, if I'd called out to them. But either they or I might as well have been American burying beetles, for all the connection we actually shared.

Then it happened.

One minute I was just sitting there, staring blankly out at our tree's empty branches and the empty sidewalk, in the gap between students passing by. In the next moment strong arms were scooping me up, and a voice was hissing, "Shh! Shh! Don't make a sound!"

I could have screamed. I had time, before the hand clamped over my mouth, before I was hustled down the stairs, before my mind clouded over with panic and other voices. But I dare you: You try, if you're ever kidnapped, to do the exact right thing at the exact right time. You try it in regular life, when you might have all the time in the world to think and plan. Sometimes you just make mistakes.

I didn't scream. I let my body go limp, which probably made it much easier to stuff me into the car waiting in the alley.

"Put her in the back. I'll drive—yes, there—hurry . . ."

I couldn't be sure I really heard them conversing. Or conspiring. Whatever. There was so much else echoing in my head, so many other conversations distracting me:

That poor girl. Do you think she's going to be all right?

. . . anything else we could do to help?

. . . I thought this essay . . .

And those bangs! Can you believe that hair? . . .

You know, the youngest . . .

I couldn't have said what was real and immediate and right there, before my very ears, and what was dim and distant and not exactly relevant at the moment. Then the hand came off my mouth and someone was pushing my face toward the cracked vinyl seat—pushing rather gently, actually, for a kidnapper.

"Sorry," a voice said. "You're going to have to keep your head down until we're out of town."

The hand slipped back over my mouth. The car lurched forward, but slowly, like it was barely creeping through the gravel alley. I could tell when we reached pavement—at the corner of Vine Street—because the car whipped dramatically to the right and sped up with a screech of the tires.

"Careful!" the voice beside me called out. "Remember, Springdale's a speed trap!"

This struck me as funny—kidnappers worrying about a speeding ticket?—but the car slowed slightly.

"Nobody's following us, are they?" the driver asked.

From my position with my face smashed against the vinyl, I could tell that the boy holding my mouth shut had turned around to look out the rear window.

Boy, I thought dazedly. *It's two boys who are kidnapping me.* I felt strangely proud, that I could think my own thoughts, despite all the other noise in my head. Despite being kidnapped.

The car slowed—because of the traffic light at the corner of Vine and Liberty, I guessed—and then veered left.

"No! That's the way they'd expect us to go!" the boy beside me exploded.

"Okay, okay. Let me think—"

"Go out 643!"

The car made a U-turn, with more screeching tires and a little wobble that made me wonder if the whole thing might just flip over. I hadn't been in a car in a while, but I did remember seat belts. I wanted a seat belt. Maybe if I asked nicely, if I promised to keep crouching down, the kidnappers would let me wear one?

Just then the boy holding on to me let go.

"Yee-ha!" he yelled. "We did it!"

I turned my head slightly and opened one eyelid a crack—

I had just then realized I'd had both eyes squeezed tightly shut. The boy was pumping his fists in the air, cheering, like someone in the pep section at the Springdale College football games. Except this boy looked too young to be in college. He was thin, the way a lot of teenagers are when they've grown so quickly they can't eat enough to keep up. He had chin-length brown hair that was a little bit straggly— his ears stuck out on the sides. And he had a kind face. I say that even though he'd just kidnapped me: You could just look at him and know he'd never kicked a dog, probably never even killed a fly.

"Are you all right?" the boy said. "You can sit up now— it's safe. We're out of Springdale. You're free. We rescued you!" He beamed at me, a beatific smile, like an angel's in an art book.

"Where would you like us to take you?" the boy in the driver's seat asked from the front. "I've got my cell phone. Is there someone you want to call?"

Granted, I'd never been kidnapped before, but it struck me that those probably weren't typical kidnapper questions. I would have answered, except that one of the voices in my head said just then, *Oh, I hate this one! That little girl is such a brat.*

"Here," the boy beside me said, lifting my head from the seat. He did it too quickly, given that my face had been plastered there for so long. I moaned with the pain of my skin peeling away from the vinyl.

"Oh, no!" the boy said. "Are you all right? I'm sorry, I'm sorry. . . . Really, there's no reason to be scared. Do you want something to drink? We've got some cans of Pepsi somewhere in here. . . ." He was lifting my shoulders, propping me up, even as he scanned the floor for the promised Pepsis. "Darnell, I think she's in shock or something. She's just . . ."

The car eased over onto the side of the road, rolling onto gravel. We were out in the country now. Springdale's small enough that you're in the country after about ten minutes in any direction. The driver had very responsibly switched on his flashing emergency lights so that anyone driving past could avoid hitting him. Some small, overly analytical part of my brain thought, *Look, guys, if you're going to make a go at being kidnappers, you really shouldn't draw attention to yourselves like that.*

But no one was driving by. No headlights swept into the car, not even from far down the road.

"Oh, no. We did scare you, didn't we?" the driver said, turning around to face me. In the scant reflected glow of the emergency lights, I could see only that his hair was as shaggy as his friend's, but blonder. "Look, we're on your side. We just wanted to save you from your father."

"My . . . father?" I choked out. The word stuck in my throat. It was difficult to say.

"Well, yeah," the boy beside me said. "We know who you are. We know all about you."

I let that pass, even though it couldn't be true.

"Look," the driver said, picking up something from the seat beside him. He passed back a newspaper clipping—no, not exactly a newspaper clipping. A *tabloid* clipping. He obligingly turned on the car's overhead light (making us more conspicuous, I'm sure) and shook out the wrinkles in the paper. Then he handed it to me.

I looked down at it, forcing my eyes to focus, to read. The headline said:

FORMER CHILD STAR HELD HOSTAGE *BY FANATIC DAD*

Down below, there was smaller type:

NOT EVEN ALLOWED TO WATCH *TV*!

I blinked, my vision swinging in and out of focus. I reminded myself that I'd known how to read perfectly well since I was four, so it shouldn't be that much of a struggle to go on, to keep reading. I gulped and launched myself into the article itself:

> Everyone knows that Lindsay Scott, former child star of the TV hit series *Just Me and the Kids*, vanished from Hollywood five years ago, when *Kids* was canceled. Now our crack investigative team has discovered that the blame lies with her fanatical father, a failed college professor with bizarre ideas about the "evils" of the modern world.

"Failed"? I thought. *"Failed"?* I winced, gasped for air, and went on.

Poor Lindsay is now virtually a prisoner in her home, rarely leaving the tiny house, and then only under the supervision of her father.

"You've got to wonder about that family," said one neighbor, who was completely unaware of Lindsay's true identity. "I lived here two years before I even knew there was a daughter. The first time I saw her face in the window, I thought it was a ghost."

Lindsay's father, Arthur Scott Curran, has taught literature, history, and "American studies" at several colleges around the country. And he's published numerous essays longing for a return to "simpler days" and "less obsession with technology rather than face-to-face human interaction." Which is strange, given that he barely allows his famous daughter to see anyone face-to-face.

"Her father?" said Daniel DeLarue, who directed Lindsay in *Just Me and the Kids.* "He was an odd bird. Only met him once or twice. Whatever the opposite of a stage parent is, that was him. He was never on the set."

Experts theorize that sometimes parents of famous children become jealous, and even attempt to punish their children for their success. Curran's unusual views make some wonder why he allowed his daughter to work in Hollywood in the first place. His essays complain about, among other things, TV, Internet dating, cell phone plans, the interstate highway system, and bikinis.

Ironically, given his daughter's career, he once wrote, "I would never allow a television in my home!"

The connection between Curran's obscure writings and his famous daughter has gone unnoticed all these years because she never used her father's name professionally.

There was more—mainly a recap of Lindsay Scott's acting career, and some of the more famous moments of *Just Me and the Kids*, I guessed—but my eyes were suddenly too blurry to read on.

No! I thought sternly. *You will not cry! You will not cry! You will not cry!* I forced my mind into analytical mode. *Literary criticism,* I told myself. *You will analyze this article for theme, bias, grammatical correctness . . .*

Anyone would be able to tell that this article came from a tabloid rather than a reputable newspaper, because there was no mention of an actual location for Lindsay Scott's "tiny house." And both the neighbor and psychological "experts" were unnamed. And "American studies" was in quotation marks, as if it were something dangerously suspect.

"Well?" the boy beside me said, as if he were sure I'd had enough time to digest the entire article. "That is you, isn't it?"

He sounded anxious, uncertain suddenly. If I just said no, would they turn around and take me home?

But the other boy answered for me.

"Toby! Of course that's her! That's her house!"

For the first time I noticed that there were two pictures

with the article. They were both blurry, black and white, poorly reproduced.

But one of the pictures was definitely of my house.

It had been taken in the wintertime, I decided, because the yard was a vague, shapeless gray—the aftermath of that snowstorm in February, probably, when the snow lingered for weeks, losing its white purity, turning dingier by the day. The day the snow fell, I'd stood in the backyard, my face upturned, staring into the swirl of flakes, shutting out everything else. By the fifth day, though, I'd stopped looking out the window.

The house itself, in the picture, looked even more rundown than usual and in need of a good coat of paint. If I squinted, I could just make out the stacks of books and papers threatening to overtake the front windows from the inside. The front steps—monumental dividing lines for me, delineating one world from another—looked inconsequential. Maybe they were partially hidden by the snow?

"We knew it was your house," the boy beside me— Toby?—started explaining, "because we saw it when we were delivering furniture in Springdale."

"We deliver all sorts of things," the boy from the front, Darnell, contributed. "After school and on weekends."

"We're the only delivery guys in the whole county, really," Toby said.

"Well, who else would do it? The pay sucks," Darnell said.

I got the feeling the two of them were used to finishing each other's sentences.

"So we saw your house, and I was like, 'Whoa, hit the brake, Darnell!'"

"No—you jerked your foot over and hit the brake yourself—idiot! We're lucky that couch we were carrying didn't flip off the back of the pickup!" Darnell corrected.

Toby shrugged, acknowledging guilt or luck, one or the other.

"See, I was really in love with you when I was about ten years old," Toby said.

I must have recoiled at that, because suddenly Toby was holding his hands up, a gesture of innocence.

"No, no, it's not like that!" he said anxiously. "I mean— that's why I wanted to save you. We're not stalkers or anything. Well, we did keep coming past your house after that, but it was just to see if you needed any help . . . and then we saw you the other night, looking out your window, and we were sure it was you, and you just looked so . . . sad."

I wasn't sure which night he meant, but I knew how I would have looked.

"Not nearly as happy as you used to be," Darnell added from the front. He pointed at the other picture, the one inset below the picture of my house. It was an official publicity shot of Lindsay Scott, the actress, aged about eleven. The girl in the picture was pretty and dark-haired, with clear skin and even features, but that wasn't what was most striking about the photo. What really stood out was her confidence. That grin on her face all but spoke, *I am so in control of my own life. I know everything I need to know. Right now.*

Which was so ironic I could barely stand to think about it.

"You think I still . . . look like that?" I mumbled.

And regretted it instantly, because wasn't that "still" an admission? Didn't it shut out the possibility that I could firmly say, "I'm not her. You have the wrong person. Take me home"?

I regretted it too because Toby flinched a little. He was going to lie.

"Well, sure," he said. "You're just older and . . ."

"Sadder," Darnell added.

"So that's why you thought I needed help?" I asked, with a steely edge to my voice. I was thinking, *I can still act, after all.*

I saw then that Toby had just started to stretch his hand toward me. Why? To pat my back? To stroke my hair? To touch my face? To comfort me? At my first word he jerked his hand back, and I was so tempted to say, "No, wait! It's okay! Go ahead! Comfort me!"

But I would have cried if I'd tried to say any of those words.

"Look," I said, straightening up, trying to muster up whatever fake Lindsay Scott confidence I could still carry off. "This is all a mistake. My father is not holding me hostage."

My voice wavered on the word "father."

Toby and Darnell stared at me, befuddlement reflected in both sets of eyes.

"You're saying that's all a lie?" Darnell asked, gesturing toward the article.

"Well . . ." I hesitated a fraction of a second too long. What amazed me most about the article was how much of it was accurate—while being completely wrong about everything that actually mattered. I finally settled for, "You know how supermarket tabloids like to twist the truth."

Their eyes were boring into me now, painfully. It'd been a long time since anybody had watched me that carefully. I couldn't take it. I looked down.

"What do you think, Toby?" Darnell said softly, as if he thought they could carry on a private conversation right in front of me.

I could *feel* Toby still watching me, trying to read my body language: the slump of my shoulder, the hair slipping down to hide my face. I made myself square my shoulders, shake my hair back, put on a brave facade. But I didn't quite dare to look directly at either one of them.

"What if it's that stockyards syndrome thing?" Toby asked.

"Huh?" Darnell asked.

"You know—I saw this show on TV. Sometimes people who are kidnapped or imprisoned or whatever start sympathizing with the people holding them captive," Toby said. "Even when they have a chance to escape, they don't."

"You mean you think she's sympathizing with *us*?" Darnell asked.

"No—with her dad," Toby said, sounding annoyed that Darnell didn't get it. "That'd be why she didn't run away on her own, even though he didn't have her chained up or anything."

I wished I'd thought before to mention the lack of chains, ropes, locks, or anything else holding me captive—anything visible, anyway. Both boys were looking at me too doubtfully for me to press that point now.

"But why's it called 'stockyards syndrome'?" Darnell asked.

"I don't know—I guess animals on their way to be killed at the stockyards act like they sympathize with the farmers?" Toby said.

There was something about being kidnapped—even by boys who didn't exactly seem like cold-blooded criminals—that made me cringe at the word "killed."

I forced myself to raise my head.

"It's 'Stockholm,'" I said. "*Stockholm* syndrome, like the city in Sweden. Not *stockyards.*" I drew in a deep breath, drawing upon all my rusty acting skills to try to sound calm and rational, and unaffected by any syndrome. "And I don't have Stockholm syndrome, so, thank you very much, but I don't need saving. Just take me home. Now."

My voice cracked—no, it splintered. *A thousand points of light,* I thought, remembering a phrase one of my father's political science professor friends liked to quote. *Only, I just revealed a thousand points of pain.*

Neither boy reacted right away.

"Oh, shoot," Toby finally said.

"What?" I said, the word wobbly and anguished, my mouth barely able to form the sounds.

"Well, how can we tell if you have stockyards—I mean

Stockholm—syndrome or not? Are you upset because we kidnapped you or because you know, deep down, that your father's a terrible man but you don't want to admit it?" Toby asked.

He had such steady brown eyes. His was the kind of gaze that a girl could drown in—not me, not any real girl, but the flighty fictional ones who inhabited the cheesy romance novels my babysitters were always leaving around the house when I was little.

I shook my head, trying to clear it.

"Why can't you just believe me?" I asked. "I don't have Stockholm syndrome! I'm not lying to you!"

Even if my professional acting skills hadn't been rusty, I'm not sure I could have carried that off. Not when I was mentally adding qualifiers: *Not lying directly, anyway. Only lies of omission, and they don't really count, do they?*

Toby and Darnell looked even more doubtful.

"Well . . . ," Toby said.

"Maybe . . . ," Darnell said.

I could tell neither of them was a fast decision maker.

"Roz would know what to do," Toby said finally.

"She doesn't get off work until nine, and what are we going to do until then?" Darnell asked. "Where can we go?"

"The Party Barn?" Toby offered.

Let me just say that not watching TV or movies for the previous five years hadn't exactly stunted my imagination about how bad things could happen to teenage girls at places with names like The Party Barn. Yes, Dad had been the one to choose most of my library books since we'd moved to Springdale, but he hadn't been into sheltering my literary taste. He'd brought me *The Lovely Bones, Freaky Green Eyes, Speak.*

It was so much easier to keep thinking about books—fiction—than to figure out how I could talk them out of taking me to that Party Barn place.

"Home," I said. "Take me home."

Toby was still watching me, his eyes narrowed. He was concentrating hard. School probably didn't come easily to him; he didn't seem like someone who trusted himself to come up with the right answers.

"Nope," he finally said, shaking his head slowly. "This is what we've got to do."

I did think, then, about jerking open the car door and jumping out. I thought, *I should have done that as soon as they stopped the car.* But I'd barely been away from my house in the past few years. The vast, dark field by the side of the road looked scarier to me than the inside of Darnell's car. Anyhow, Darnell and Toby would have been able to chase me down, to catch me. . . .

It was too late. Darnell had shifted his car out of park; he was speeding down the road. He reached one hand up to turn out the overhead light, and then the whole car was dark.

I realized I was shaking. Shivers rippled through me; my teeth chattered.

"Hey," Toby said. "Hey. It's okay. We're not going to hurt

you. I promise. Darnell—Darnell, can't you tell her something that will make her believe us?"

I scrunched over against the door, as far away from Toby as I could get. One of the voices in my head said, *Yes, that's what I'd like to do with her. And then* . . . So I couldn't hear Darnell's attempt at convincing me.

I don't know how long it took to get to the Party Barn, but it was a big, dark building in the middle of more vacant fields. Toby had to carry me in. I think I was sobbing by then—I must have been, because Toby started saying, "Oh, man, she's completely freaking out! What are we going to do?"

Darnell opened the door of the Party Barn with a key. It was a broad enclosure, clean and bright and modern. A place that shouldn't have had any ghosts or ghostly voices.

But I could still hear an echo in my mind: *Oh, that Lindsay* . . .

"See, it's a safe place," Toby was saying. "People rent it out for family reunions and 4-H events and church picnics and . . ." He must have seen me looking at a big-screen TV in the center of a cluster of couches. "And football parties. You know."

I didn't know. Family reunions and 4-H events and church picnics and football parties weren't part of my life.

Toby placed me gently on one of the couches.

"Look," he said. "We'll just go. You'll be fine here by yourself. And then we'll come back with Roz, and she'll know what to do."

Incredibly, he was tucking a comforter around my shoulders. And then he and Darnell must have tiptoed out, because when I opened my eyes again, they were gone.

I could still hear them, though. I could still hear their voices, loud and clear and worried: *Oh, man, we really messed up. Now what are we going to do?*

Chapter 2

I must have fallen asleep, because the next thing I knew I was waking up with my hands clutched over my ears, my face mashed into the comforter, my shoulders hunched up defensively. I was waking up because a strange girl was crouched down beside me, gingerly touching my arm.

"Hello?" she said. "Uh—Lindsay?"

I opened both eyes and jerked back, away from her hand.

"Okay," she said, in the same forced-calm tone the animal trainers used to use on the set. "It's okay."

She leaned back, giving me space. I half-sat up, and for a moment the two of us just stared at each other.

Roz, I thought groggily. *She's got to be Roz.*

Roz had blunt-cut chin-length dark hair—very business-like—but part of it was pulled up messily into a sort of topknot ponytail. She had on jeans and a maroon T-shirt that said STRALEY'S FAMILY DINER on the pocket. She smelled like french fries. And something about the set of her jaw and the tilt of her head made me remember what Toby and Darnell had said about her: "Roz would know what to do."

"Okay," Roz said. "Here's the thing. If I had half a brain, I'd be acting all surprised right now—'Oh, my gosh! Who are you? What are you doing here?'—and I'd be doing everything to pretend I don't even know Toby and Darnell. But everybody knows I've been bailing those two idiots out of trouble ever since kindergarten, so . . ." She shrugged. "I'll tell you the truth. I'm cleaning up their mess once again."

"I'm the 'mess'?" I asked.

I meant my words to come out sounding ironic and hip and cool. It was like I wanted Roz to be able to go back to Toby and Darnell and tell them, "Wow, that Lindsay Scott— you were completely wrong. She wasn't freaking out. We're talking, like, nerves of steel."

My voice broke on the word "mess."

"It's not your fault," Roz said. "And they mean well, they really do. But . . ." She shrugged and held up a key ring containing a shimmering silver key. "Here's what we're going to do. I sent Toby and Darnell away, because they said you were scared of them. I don't want you to be scared. So— here." She dropped the key into my lap. "You can drive my car. You'll be in control. And you can go wherever you want—back to your house, to the bus station in Rantoul, to the police. Anywhere. I don't think I have enough gas to get to Chicago, but—hey. I could make Toby and Darnell pay."

I looked down at the key, temptation itself. For a minute I pictured myself at some anonymous bus station, maybe striding confidently through O'Hare airport. Getting away.

No. It wouldn't work.

"I can't drive," I whispered.

"All right," Roz said briskly.

I was a little disappointed that she didn't seem surprised. Did I look that pathetic? Everybody expects normal red-blooded American teenagers to be clamoring for their driver's licenses the minute they turn sixteen. I'd been sixteen for months. Didn't I look normal?

"Do you trust me to drive you, then, or do you want to call someone for a ride?" Roz offered.

I considered this, though it really wasn't much of a choice.

"You," I finally mumbled.

"Come on, then," Roz said, standing up.

I let the comforter slip from my shoulders, and Roz bent over to pick it up. She folded it into a precise square and put it back on the couch.

"This way," Roz said.

She led me out the same door Toby had carried me through only—what? an hour? two hours earlier? She turned out the lights behind us. I stumbled in the gravel outside, and she caught my arm.

"Careful," she said.

"I know," I said. "I just . . ."

I couldn't finish the thought. Couldn't explain. Couldn't think straight.

Roz steadied me and helped me into her car. It was a little car, so old and decrepit-looking you wouldn't have thought it could still run. She must have seen me looking doubtful, because she rolled her eyes.

"Yeah, it's held together with duct tape and baling wire. I was probably overstating things, saying I could take you to Chicago. Sorry."

"I just want to go home," I murmured.

Roz stopped for a moment, her forehead braced against her arms, which were folded against the roof of the car.

"That's cool," she said, and let out a deep breath.

She'd circled the car and slipped into the driver's seat before I figured out what that meant.

"You were afraid," I said. "Right? Afraid I was going to go to the police?"

She shot me a sidelong glance as she backed up.

"You still could," she said evenly.

"But you don't want me to," I said.

She frowned, her eyes trained on the gravel lane ahead.

"It's up to you," she said carefully. Then she winced. "Look, I told them I wasn't going to defend them. They really screwed up this time. You'd be within your rights to go to the police, to sue. . . . I mean, this is the kind of thing people get sent to jail for! And I'll probably look like an accessory to the crime. But . . ."

"What?" I said.

"Couldn't you tell they thought they were helping?" Roz said. "They're like little puppies peeing on the carpet by mistake—no, wait, that's not the right analogy. They're like . . . like little puppies who dig up your whole flower bed, the one you just finished planting, and they come to you with a mouthful of wilted, dying flowers, and their little puppy dog eyes are all, like, 'Look what I did for you! I love you so much!' and you're just so *furious* with them, but at the same time, you can't really stay mad, because you know they don't understand. You know they were trying to do something good."

From the way she told that story, I thought she probably had a puppy. But I noticed that I'd moved down on the analogy scale.

"So I'm dog pee now?" I asked. "And wilted flowers?"

Even on the dark gravel lane, I could tell that she was gripping the steering wheel so tightly her knuckles showed white.

"It's not a perfect comparison," she said, her voice steady and calm. "The point is, Toby and Darnell didn't mean to do anything wrong."

I settled back into my seat, wishing I could clear my mind.

Focus . . .

There was a glow-in-the-dark smiley face sticker on the dashboard, and a plastic Hawaiian lei hanging from the rearview mirror. Beyond the dashboard, beyond the lei, the countryside flashed by, monotonous fields broken only occasionally by farmhouses and barns.

In a few months they'll be planting corn in those fields, I told myself, clutching at something resembling a normal thought. *Corn. Soybeans. Wheat.*

I cleared my throat.

"I know Toby and Darnell didn't mean any harm," I said carefully. "I heard them. Talking. When they didn't think I was listening."

I wanted to let them off the hook, let Roz off the hook. I didn't blame them for anything. If I were that simple Lindsay Scott from the tabloid article—the one whose only problem was a fanatical, restrictive father—I probably would have been delighted to be kidnapped.

Unless I did have "stockyards" syndrome.

I started giggling.

"What?" Roz said.

"Nothing," I said.

Giggling probably wasn't appropriate behavior for someone who'd just been kidnapped and was now in the midst of being un-kidnapped. But I couldn't stop. And then suddenly the giggles weren't giggles; they were tears again.

"Hey," Roz said.

I got a hold of myself. Literally. I clutched my arms together over my chest, holding back giggles and tears. All forms of emotion.

"It's been a long night," I said.

Roz nodded, but she was peering at me with great concern.

"I'll be fine as soon as I get home," I added.

A few more vacant fields flew by in the dark.

"Is—well, your dad—I mean—" Roz, who'd handled this whole un-kidnapping so calmly, seemed suddenly tongue-tied.

"Don't worry. He won't go to the police either," I said coldly.

Roz grimaced.

"I was kind of worried about you, too," she said. "He wouldn't . . . hurt you or anything, would he? He wouldn't think you just ran away?"

I tried to think what I could say that wouldn't be a lie, a half lie, an implied lie, or such a complete, unmitigated falsehood that it could trip me up in the next ten minutes while I was sitting in Roz's car.

"You've got nothing to worry about," I finally said, putting a little too much emphasis on the "You." *I, on the other hand . . .*

I stared at the glow-in-the-dark smiley face. Smiley faces were weird, I decided. How could two dots and a curve encompass the vastness of happiness? Really, symbols in general were inadequate. So were analogies, comparisons of any kind.

This was getting too close to ideas that belonged to other people, people I didn't want to think about just then. I squinted at the glow of the horizon, the first glimmer of the Springdale city limits.

Roz said something, but I missed it. She tried again when we pulled up to the first stoplight.

"How do I get to your house?"

"Um, go straight until you're past the college."

I had to be careful directing her through my hometown, a place I'd barely even seen. Mostly, traveling through Springdale, I always had my teeth clenched, my face scrunched up in concentration, my every muscle tensed. That didn't contribute to my being able to pay close attention to street signs and landmarks.

"Turn here," I said, right after the college student center flashed by. "No—sorry—next light . . ."

And then, quickly, we were pulling up in front of my house. My bedroom window was still hanging wide open, the old-fashioned white lace curtains blowing back and forth in the breeze. One light glowed dimly in the living room.

"This one?" Roz said.

"Yeah. Thanks."

I had the door open and was heading up the sidewalk practically before the car stopped moving. *The doorstep . . . if I can just make it to the doorstep . . .*

I realized Roz had gotten out of the car and was following me. Maybe I was staggering a little: She had her arms spread wide, like she thought she might have to catch me.

I reached the doorstep. Safety. Silence. Protection. I was home free. I whirled on Roz.

"Really, thanks for everything you did," I said, my voice firm and resolute. I felt so clearheaded now; I could focus on every word I spoke. "I do appreciate it. And tell Toby and Darnell I have no intention of going to the police. Just tell them not to kidnap anybody else."

"Oh, believe me, I—," Roz began. But I was already wrestling the door open—it wasn't even locked.

"Thanks," I said quickly, and slipped inside.

Maybe I slammed the door right in Roz's face. I couldn't be held responsible. I was just so relieved to be home.

The knocking began almost immediately.

Chapter 3

It was Roz, of course. I didn't really have to look out the peephole, but I did anyway. She was standing on the doorstep, pounding her fists against the wood door, hard enough that it had to hurt.

"Wait, Lindsay, I still wanted to talk to you," she hollered between knocks.

I turned the lock on the doorknob. Locking myself in. Locking her out.

"No need," I shouted back through the door. "Everything's fine now. No sweat."

"Please?" she yelled.

"Go away!" I yelled back.

Abruptly the knocking stopped. I peeked out—the doorstep was empty.

I sank down into my father's reading chair by the door.

The silence in my house was so pure, so blessed. I felt cleansed. I let my head fall forward into my hands, letting the stress flow out of me.

Relax. It's over. Don't think about any of it.

I heard footsteps upstairs.

A second later Roz appeared at the top of the stairs. The stairs indoors. She was inside my house.

I stared at her, speechless.

"Okay, I just proved that I'm every bit as stupid as Toby and Darnell," she said as she descended the stairs. "Is breaking and entering as serious a crime as kidnapping?"

"You came in my bedroom window," I said incredulously.

"Yeah, well, it was open, so I guess you could only have me arrested for trespassing. Entering, without the breaking—does that reduce my sentence?" She sounded nervous. She was biting her lip, rubbing her hands through her messy ponytail, bringing down strands of hair to swing into her face.

"Why?" I said. "Why'd you—" I waved my hands before me, indicating her presence. The gesture finished the sentence for me.

"I have to talk to you," Roz said in a low, urgent voice. "Something's wrong."

I realized I'd underestimated Roz. If Toby and Darnell were like eager misguided puppies, Roz had her canine tendencies too. She was like a bulldog. Tenacious.

I forced myself to throw off a casual-sounding laugh.

"Yeah, what's wrong is that I was *kidnapped* tonight," I said. "Not the most pleasant experience, even if it was a mistake."

Roz reached the bottom of the stairs now. She stood there, in front of the wood post, staring hard at me.

"There's something you're not telling me," she said.

I reached back into my memory, trying to remember how to arrange my face into that wide-eyed innocent look the director always liked me to have on *Just Me and the Kids.* A look that was completely fake by the end.

"Something I'm not telling you?" I mimicked incredulously. "I don't even *know* you! Why would I tell you anything?"

Roz tapped her finger on her chin.

"That Party Barn?" she said. "Where Toby and Darnell left you? When I got there, the door wasn't locked. You could have left. Or, if you'd walked into the kitchenette, you would have found a phone on the wall. You could have called anybody on the planet."

Roz was watching too carefully for my reaction. I tried not to let my face change too much.

"Really?" I said. I raised my eyebrows in what the *Kids* director used to call an "Aw, shucks, the joke's on me" expression. Usually I hadn't had to make that expression. Usually it was one of the other kids.

"Really," Roz said. "Even if there wasn't a phone, even if the door was locked—you could have broken a window. You could have escaped, easy. *Most* people would have."

I made myself keep staring right back at her.

"I guess I can join the stupid club with you and Toby and Darnell," I said. "Too bad."

Roz's gaze was intense now.

"Why didn't you try to escape?" she asked in a soft voice. "Why?"

"I told you," I said. "I knew Toby and Darnell weren't going to hurt me." *Had* I told her that? It was hard to remember exactly what I'd said in the car. "And . . . I wasn't thinking clearly. Because of being kidnapped."

Roz kept peering at me intently.

"Are you on drugs?" she asked.

"*No,*" I said, indignant. "What, you think just because I was on TV—you think it's required? Stardom by ten, rehab by twenty?"

"Well, that is a pretty common pattern," Roz muttered.

I think she meant for me to laugh at that, but I didn't. I sat up straight and stared back at her. Defiant.

"Not for me," I said.

"Toby and Darnell said you were acting weird," Roz said.

"I was being kidnapped!"

"And then you were still kind of acting weird when you were in my car," Roz went on, as if she hadn't heard me. "But now you're . . . different. If you were on something, it's worn off."

I decided Roz wasn't asking about the drugs just because I'd been a child actor. I could see her with somebody at her school, intervening like that, asking point-blank, "Are you on drugs?" She'd be the caring, compassionate friend, the one who'd deliver the "just say no" lecture.

I'd been on a couple of after-school specials. I knew how these things worked.

I stood up. I faced her squarely. Acting again.

"I didn't realize there was a code of conduct for people being kidnapped," I said, actually managing a sarcastic twist to my words. "Act one way, it's normal. Act another way, it'll look like you're on drugs. What is this, blame the victim?"

I was proud of my improvisation.

But Roz was looking past me, her eyes taking in the stacks of books on the floor and table. And—I gazed around too—she was probably also noticing the layers of dust on the stacks of books, and everywhere else. What can I say? I'd had lots of other things to think about lately.

"You didn't even call anybody when you got home," Roz said, half to herself. "No, 'Hi, Mom. Hi, Dad. Everything's fine now, but . . .' No urgent cell call to your friends, 'Guess what just happened to me?'"

She was making me feel very, very lonely.

Would normal people have that? Someone to comment to about everything? Someone who wouldn't talk, necessarily, but would just . . . listen?

Roz had stepped slightly past me, and was looking at the wall. It was almost as if she thought the framed photos of nineteenth-century Springdale were actually interesting. Then she whirled around.

"I need to talk to your father," she said firmly.

"What?" This was not what I'd expected. Panic bubbled up in my stomach. "You can't! I mean—a few minutes ago you thought he might hurt me." I was proud of myself for hitting on this excuse so quickly. "Do you *want* to get me in trouble?"

Roz regarded me calmly.

"I don't think that's what's going on here," she said. "You don't sound like you're scared of your father."

I bit my lip.

"He's not here," I said. "English professors have office hours on Wednesday nights."

These were two absolutely true facts. Also, absolutely unrelated.

Roz pulled a cell phone out of her back pocket.

"What's his number?" she asked, fingers poised over the keys.

She's bluffing, I thought. *Isn't she?*

"I'm not going to tell you," I said, my chin jutting up into the air.

"Fine," Roz said. She punched numbers on the phone and put it to her ear. "Campus information?" she said. "Could I have the office number for a professor, uh—"

"You don't even know his name!" I taunted.

She ignored me.

"Arthur Scott Curran?" she said into the phone.

Toby and Darnell must have shown her the tabloid article. She must have paid attention.

I watched her face, wondering what she was going to hear. Springdale was a tiny college; everybody knew everything. Or thought they did, anyway. But maybe Roz had gotten some brand-new campus information operator, someone who didn't know about my father and would just read off numbers that were probably still in the computer system.

Roz's whole expression shifted suddenly. Because I didn't want to think about certain other things, I thought about earthquakes, about cataclysmic meteors slamming into the ground, wiping out entire species. *That's* how much her face changed.

"Are you sure?" she asked. Long silence. The operator must have been giving her a long answer. "No, thank you," Roz finally said, lowering the phone from her ear.

She looked back at me, her gaze a strange mix of accusation and sympathy.

"Your father's dead?" she whispered.

Chapter 4

I slumped back into my father's chair. Certain words . . .
I wonder how many times you have to hear them before
they lose their power. I felt, *again*, like I'd been punched in
the gut. I felt, *again*, like that punch had knocked out huge
chunks of myself, and maybe there wasn't any part of me
left intact.

Just when I thought I'd been doing better.

I realized that I hadn't answered Roz.

"It's true?" she asked.

I nodded, looking down.

"Toby and Darnell would have known that," I muttered.
"If they'd read the *Springdale Messenger* instead of the *National Enquirer* or wherever that article was from."

My father's obituary had been in the local newspaper. It
was very short, and not very detailed, but still.

"That *article*," Roz gasped. "About your 'fanatical father' . . .
Gah." She seemed to be choking on the horror of it all. "And

then you had to read that . . . Don't tabloids check any of their facts?"

"He was still alive when that article was written," I whispered. "I looked at the date. He . . . died the next day."

"Why didn't you tell Toby and Darnell?"

My head shot up.

"Oh, right, that sounds like great advice for someone being kidnapped," I said sarcastically. "Tell the kidnappers you're home alone, tell them you've got no one watching out for you, tell them nobody cares if you live or die . . ." I was surprised at the venom in my voice.

"That can't be true," Roz murmured. She still looked stunned. "Surely your mother . . . ?"

"She's gone. I haven't seen her in years."

In a weird way I was enjoying this. It was like a game the other kids and I used to play on the set, Gross Out, where we competed to tell the most disgusting stories. Only now I was trying for the most horrifying effect. What could I say to make Roz's eyes bug out even more?

Roz blinked.

"Then who do you live with?" she asked, challenging me. "You're what—sixteen? They don't let sixteen-year-olds live alone."

Oops. I'd gone too far. I forgot that this wasn't just a game.

"Mrs. Mullin—she's the English department secretary—she's been taking care of me," I said. "And I'm starting college early. In the summer—just a few months away."

I shrugged with just the right level of carelessness to dismiss being a sixteen-year-old, to dismiss childhood altogether. Ordinary mortals might still need adult supervision at sixteen, but not Lindsay Scott.

"Then that Mrs. Mullin—she's the person I should talk to about you?" Roz asked.

I frowned at her.

"Roz, *please*," I said. "Mrs. Mullin and my father were . . . close." I made it sound like the two of them had been having an affair. I was acting again. If I pulled this off, I would deserve an Oscar. "She was the one who found his body, so, as you can understand, she's very upset about everything. I'm home now, I'm fine. . . . If you talk to her and say anything about Toby and Darnell trying to kidnap me, it will just make her more upset. She'll feel guilty for not . . . protecting me. So, please. Drop it."

Roz tilted her head. For a long moment I was in doubt: *Does she believe me or not?* But then she gave me a sympathetic half smile.

"Okay," Roz said. "I'm sorry. I'm sorry about everything. I'll just . . . go."

"You can use the door," I said. "You don't have to go out the way you came in."

I grinned, making the joke, taking control. *Oh, I am smooth.*

"Sorry," Roz said again, reaching for the door handle. She gave it a twist and a jerk and let herself out.

And then I was completely alone.

Chapter 5

I stood at the window watching Roz back away from the curb in her car held together with duct tape and baling wire. I told myself I was only making sure that she really did leave, that she wasn't going to come creeping back down the stairs again when I least expected it. Still, I felt an odd lurch in my stomach when her headlights swung around the corner, out of sight.

She was gone.

Good, I told myself, and just to prove how relieved I was I went upstairs and slammed my bedroom window down, shutting out the whole world.

Coming back out of my bedroom, I came face-to-face with the door of my father's room.

It's just a door, I told myself. *Just an inanimate panel of wood. It doesn't have a face.*

Still.

My father's chosen area of study had been transcendentalism. I'd always tried to tune him out every time he talked about it—about how all sorts of ordinary things are full of deep meaning, and intuition trumps rationality, and everything is symbolic, blah, blah, blah, blah, blah. But evidently I'd absorbed enough that I couldn't quite believe that the door was just an inanimate panel of wood. It seemed perfectly capable of beckoning to me, chastising me, sympathizing with me. I reached out and clutched the door handle, turned it, gave the door a little shove. It creaked open half an inch.

"Dad?" I whispered.

Did I expect an answer?

There wasn't one. But then, even if my dad had been alive and well and sitting in his room, he might not have answered anyhow. He actually hadn't talked to me that much about transcendentalism. Most of the time he just sat and stared at his notes, so lost in thought that he didn't see or hear me.

Here are the details you're probably wondering about:

Two weeks ago.

Heart attack.

Yes, very sudden. Completely out of the blue. One minute my father was standing in the English department mail room, taking the latest edition of *Transcendentalist Scholar* out of the box marked ADJUNCT FACULTY. And the next moment he was sprawled on the floor, dead. At least that's what everyone assumed happened. Nobody actually saw it.

My father died alone.

Mrs. Mullin, the English department secretary, was the one who found him, but it wasn't anything like the romantic/tragic moment I sort of implied to Roz. Mrs. Mullin was probably seventy years old, blue-haired, scatterbrained.

She didn't know who my father was when she found him, dead on the mail room floor.

In Mrs. Mullin's defense, the Springdale College English department employs several adjunct professors, and one slightly seedy middle-aged, balding, never-going-to-get-tenure adjunct probably looked much the same as all the others.

I can picture Mrs. Mullin, in her thirty-years-out-of-date polyester dress, stepping into the mail room, probably humming—she's a hummer—and then gasping in horror at the sight before her eyes. And then, what Mrs. Mullin told me happened next was that she got down on the floor on her arthritic knees and bent over my father's body and hugged him.

"Maybe you think I should have tried CPR instead?" she'd asked me at the funeral in her creaky old-lady's voice, her owl-like eyes magnified behind her thick glasses.

"The EMTs said he'd been dead a while," I told her over the buzzing in my head, the whirling in my mind. "It wouldn't have mattered."

"The *hug* mattered," Mrs. Mullin said fiercely, like some strict schoolmarm correcting a hopeless dunce. "That was a man who needed a hug."

So maybe Mrs. Mullin had known my father, even without knowing his name. Maybe I wasn't exactly lying to Roz when I told her Mrs. Mullin and my father had been close.

I was at home—of course I was at home—when the police came to notify my father's next of kin. Usually I didn't open the door when the bell rang and I could see it was Jehovah's Witnesses or vinyl siding salesmen or even just Girl Scouts selling cookies. I had my reasons. I thought I could avoid the police officer, too; I figured he was just asking about some neighbor's lost cat. (There's not really any crime in Springdale. My kidnapping by Toby and Darnell, if I'd reported it, would probably have gone down in Springdale records as the worst crime of the century.) But then the police officer *came in.* He used my father's key and unlocked the door and stepped into the living room.

My instincts were still to hide: I stepped out the back door. But in my haste I stepped a little too far, and suddenly I knew. I knew exactly what the police officer had come to tell me.

I stood there devastated, unable to move, a girl turned to stone.

"Miss?" the police officer said behind me.

When I was on *Just Me and the Kids,* the girl who played my older sister, Olivia Jerome, was always breaking up with her boyfriend or getting dumped by her boyfriend or finding out that her boyfriend was cheating on her with her best friend. So she'd show up at the studio with tears streaming down her face behind the tinted glass of her limousine.

Past the paparazzi, she'd walk in looking like tragedy personified, Young Woman Ruined Forever. But somehow, by the time Daniel called "Action!" she'd be transformed into bubbleheaded, carefree Susie Lou, grinning from ear to ear. Toward the end, when I had devastation of my own to deal with, I asked Olivia her secret, and—though I couldn't trust her otherwise—she told me.

Standing there frozen in my own backyard, *knowing*, knowing entirely too much, I told myself I had to act like Olivia acting like Susie Lou.

"Oh!" I said, whirling around, my face a mask of fake surprise at the sight of the cop on our back step. "I was taking out the trash—did you ring the bell? Did you need something?"

I pretended not to notice that he'd just walked out of my house, that that should have made me suspicious. I edged back closer to the house, almost touching the peeling wood. I couldn't have continued acting like Olivia acting like Susie Lou any farther away than that.

The police officer gave me an awkward version of either a grimace or a smile—it was hard to tell what he was trying for. He had a gap between his two front teeth, and freckles across the bridge of his nose.

"Are you related to"—he had to look down at his notes. I hated him for that—"Arthur Curran?"

"He's my father," I said, allowing some puzzlement and concern into my voice.

People who might be likely to die unexpectedly should

always carry lists with them, with a ranking of who should be notified in what order in case of emergency. The cop and I spent a ridiculous amount of time dancing around the central question of who deserved to hear the bad news first.

"Is your mother home?"

"No."

"Does your mother live here?"

"No."

"Is there somewhere else I could reach your mother?"

"No. I haven't seen her in sixteen years."

"Is there some other adult in your life we could talk to?"

"You mean besides my father?"

I made myself gasp, the Olivia-as-Susie-Lou act fading into another impersonation: the girl who's not *that* stupid getting an intuition that something's really wrong.

"Did something happen to my father?" I asked, my voice breathy with anxiety. It wasn't all fake.

The cop winced. I could see he was a nice guy, probably one of those public servants who truly did see his purpose in the world as helping people. It was so clear that he didn't want to tell me anything until I had at least an aunt or a cousin—somebody!—by my side.

"Oh, please," I said. "Tell me. My father doesn't have any other family besides me."

I have to hand it to Officer Helpful. He gave it to me straight then, without any more pussyfooting around.

"Your father's dead."

And if I'd heard it just like that, without any preparation, without any bracing, without any warning, I would have fallen apart. Everything else would have flown out of my head, and I'd be in some foster home right now, slowly being buried in chatter.

As it was, I recoiled, flinched, sagged against the wall of my house.

"No," I whispered. "It can't be. But I just got home this morning from college—I was going to surprise him. . . ."

It was saying that word, "college," then, in that first moment, that made everything else work. If I'd waited until later, until it was clear that I'd had time to recover from the shock and concoct a story, someone would have investigated. Someone would have looked up my birth date, checked into my alleged college enrollment, discovered I wasn't close enough to adulthood to be trusted on my own, or to make funeral arrangements for my only remaining parent. Someone would have realized that I was every bit as young as I looked.

I even made mistakes—when the police officer asked what college I went to, I said, "Dartvard. I mean, Harmouth." But people expect you to be woozy and stupid and stuttery when you've just lost your father. I ended up fooling everyone.

Except Mrs. Mullin.

Mrs. Mullin, she of the polyester dress and too-thick eyeglasses, kept sidling over to me at the funeral—which was sparsely attended, mostly by Dad's fellow sad-sack adjuncts.

"You're not going straight back to college, are you, dear?" she asked.

"Er—no, I'm going to finish out the semester from home," I said, because I could just see her offering to watch over the house in my absence. "I only have to turn in a few essays and reports, and I can use the Springdale College library. . . . This way I'll be able to pack up Dad's papers."

She clucked her tongue.

"All by yourself?" she asked.

Someone pulled her away—Dr. Dribolt, wanting to find out about the composition schedule for the fall—but a few minutes later she was back at my side.

"Why don't you let me and my husband, Elgin, come by to help you?" Mrs. Mullin asked. "I'll bring my chicken casserole. Tomorrow? Sometime next week?"

For a split second I let myself picture what she was describing. I saw it as one of those montages they did all the time on *Kids*, to avoid showing any tedium in our fictional lives. There'd be me opening the door, my expression a mixture of dread and duty. And grief, of course. And then there'd be the three of us sitting around the dinner table, tentative at first, but then gradually drawing one another out over the home-cooked casserole, which would surely be made with cream of mushroom soup. We'd discover an amazing shared interest in, I don't know, something like needlepoint. Then we'd labor over the boxes of papers, my expression growing pensive, the thought balloon all but appearing over my head: "I may have lost my father, but there are still people who care about me." And then, inevitably, there'd be a group hug, Mr. and Mrs. Mullin symbolically drawing me into their family, since I no longer had one of my own.

This is how low I'd sunk at my father's funeral: That vision was tempting.

But I knew there'd be an "after," maybe lots of "afters." Eventually I'd regret it.

I always did.

"No, thank you, Mrs. Mullin," I said politely. "I think my father would want me to do this on my own."

Mrs. Mullin raised a penciled-in eyebrow.

"All right, then," she said reluctantly. "Let me know if you change your mind. I *will* bring the casserole, at least. A young thing like you needs to keep up her strength."

That'd been the start of it. Mrs. Mullin had stopped by to bring the casserole, and then she'd come back to pick up the dish, "to save you the trouble of having to return it, dear." And then she'd dropped off Dad's last paycheck—"It seemed so cold and heartless, just to mail it . . ." And each time, she'd looked at me more and more skeptically; each time, she'd inched closer and closer to ending the polite pretense and just blurting out, "All right, young lady. What are you trying to pull here?"

Sometimes it's the kind ones you have to worry about the most.

But I'd figured out how to solve my Mrs. Mullin problem. I figured it out right before I climbed out my bedroom window, right before Toby and Darnell snatched me off my own balcony. Solving that problem was the reason I'd been able to appreciate the spring air, been able to fully feel the change of seasons.

Yes, I could solve my Mrs. Mullin problem.

As long as Roz didn't try to talk to her.

Chapter 6

Maybe you think I've left something out of my story so far?

Maybe you're wondering how I knew my father was dead before the policeman told me?

You don't understand yet?

Later. I'll tell you later.

Chapter 7

I sat down to do my algebra homework, just like I should have before.

See, Dad? I wanted to tell him. *I'm carrying on as if you're still alive. I'm doing what you always wanted me to do.*

My father grew up in a small town—really just a crossroads—called Pine Needle, Nebraska. He was the only person from his high school graduating class to go to college. He started out at Hicksville Junior College—you probably think I'm making that up, but I'm not. From there it was one obscure cut-rate poorly ranked school after another, right up to his doctorate from Nowhere University. (Okay, okay, it was really called Undt University. But the effect's the same.)

"The sad thing is, I really thought I was going places," my dad told me once, late at night, when I found him just sitting in the living room staring out the window. "I always thought I was the smartest kid in every one of my classes."

And maybe he was. Maybe his smarts and his hard work and his willingness to live on nothing but ramen noodles would have paid off if he hadn't chosen to go into such a snobbish, overcrowded field. Or if he hadn't specialized in such a dull, narrow subject. (Transcendentalism, yes, but not for him the shining beacons of Thoreau, of Emerson. Surely you've heard of them? And yet my dad's doctoral thesis was about the completely unknown Rutherford Dunder.)

Or maybe none of that really mattered. Maybe it was my mother breaking his heart that ruined my father's life.

Who am I to know?

My father never spoke about the heartbreak. But for as long as I could remember, he'd been determined that I was going to get a better education than he'd gotten. Or a more prestigious one, anyway. I was going to go to a brand-name college, one of those that make people gasp a little, in awe. I was going to have doors opening for me, right and left, instead of constantly slamming in my face.

When I got the chance to act on *Kids*—just a happenstance, a fluke—he let me do it only because Jodie Foster got into Yale, Natalie Portman got into Harvard, Julia Stiles got into Columbia. He was never satisfied with my on-set tutor. "Tell him you want to know more than how to mouth insipid lines and count your money," he told me. "Tell him *Moby-Dick* is *not* too hard for an eight-year-old. Excerpts, anyway."

After *Kids* ended, I started taking Internet classes, far more advanced than anything a local school might offer. Next fall, when I'd take the SAT, I was supposed to achieve perfect scores. I'd already been taking practice tests.

As for the logistics of actually leaving home, actually *going* to a college campus . . .

Maybe it's merciful that my father is dead, so he won't have to see me fail?

I stabbed my pencil into my algebra homework with so much ferocity, it was like I thought I was murdering that traitorous thought.

I don't have to worry about that yet. One step at a time. All I have to think about right now is algebra. Nothing else matters.

Unless Roz was right that minute hunting up Mrs. Mullin, and they began comparing stories, finding the holes in my facade, agreeing to bring in social workers, counselors, intervention. . . .

Algebra! 6x squared minus 4x plus 5 equals . . .

I can't let them ruin everything!

I sighed and put down the pencil. I glanced toward the window behind my desk—the window I'd climbed out earlier. How easy my life had seemed then, when all I'd had to worry about was grief and algebra.

I knew what I had to do, but I was avoiding it.

This is what I get for convincing everyone I'm a grown-up. I have to act like one.

I pushed myself away from my desk, stood up, and went out into the hall. I carefully did not look at the door to my father's room. I climbed down the stairs and went into the kitchen. The clock on the stove said it was 10:53. I had seven minutes.

I took a deep breath, opened the back door, and stepped outside.

Chapter 8

I have to tell you my secret.

I can't go on with my story without revealing it. I had a pretty good run, hiding from everyone for five years. For five years I was safe. But now . . .

"Dad, this is all your fault," I muttered, perched on the back step, my head against the door.

Had I moved to a new stage in the Elisabeth Kübler-Ross cycle of grief? Did I need to indulge in long recitations of Daddy-hating Sylvia Plath poetry?

No. I needed to know what Roz was up to.

I inched forward . . . and then leaped off the back step.

Instantly I could hear.

I don't mean that I could hear a car with a bad muffler driving down Vine Street, a dog barking in a fenced yard three houses down, the faint music that always seemed to float out from frat row a few blocks over—though I could. But I could have heard any of that inside the house too, if I'd only opened the window and listened.

What I could hear in the backyard—what I could hear anywhere outside my own home—was far beyond that. I could hear sound waves that should have been too weak and far away to reach my ears. I could hear someone in Singapore, actually, though I couldn't understand what they were saying. I could hear someone in California, and someone in Kansas, and someone in Georgia. I could hear Toby. Darnell. Roz. Mrs. Mullin.

This is my secret. I would call it a hidden talent, but talents are supposed to be happy possessions, something to rejoice over and nurture and maybe even gloat about. My secret skill has brought me nothing but pain.

At any given moment I can hear anything anybody says about me, anywhere in the world.

I know because I heard the *Kids*'s director criticizing my acting ability once when I was certain he was on a Paris vacation; I heard Anthony Duzan, the father on the show, cursing me for getting more lines per episode than he did. He was in Rio de Janeiro at the time.

This is not a skill I've always had. It started when I was eleven, the day I got my first period.

That same week my face was on the cover of *People* magazine.

Do you know how petty people can be? Do you know how they'll look at a little girl's face and laugh at the tilt of her nose, the freckles on her cheeks, the one strand of hair that's out of place (that wasn't Photoshopped out, because the photo editor thought it was "cute")? Do you know how many people in this world want to do nothing but tear other people down?

And then there are the men who don't just *think* awful thoughts but talk about them . . .

Anyhow.

Now, in my backyard in Springdale, I stood with my face lifted up to the sky, and I listened to Roz's voice.

There's something going on with her I just don't understand.

Oh, come on, Roz. You understand everything.

That was Toby, I thought, answering back. Both of their voices had a scratchy staticky quality to them—were they talking by phone?

The conversation faded out momentarily, maybe because they weren't talking directly about me. Then I heard: *Toby, it's not really any of our business. She was an* actress. *She's probably got agents and accountants and all sorts of people watching out for her.*

Yeah, those sorts of people have done such a great job taking care of Lindsay Lohan and Britney Spears.

Oh, right, and your approach—kidnapping her?—that was so much smarter.

I had to smile at the sarcasm dripping from Roz's voice. Then my smile faded.

Roz, why don't you go talk to that Mrs. Mullin person? Toby was saying. *What's it going to hurt?*

At eleven o'clock at night? No way. And—Lindsay specifically asked me not to. Toby . . . I don't think you're thinking about this the right way. Just because you used to watch this girl on TV, that doesn't mean her whole life's supposed to be on display for your viewing pleasure. I think you've got a dissociative disorder or—what's it called? One of those other psychology terms I need to learn for the quiz tomorrow. Just because you watched Lindsay Scott on TV, you think you're connected. But you're not. She's nothing to you. You're nothing to her.

But don't you remember, when I was in middle school . . . This was Toby again. I had to strain to hear him. His voice sounded strangled, choked. *When my parents were fighting all the time and . . . Well, you know. Everything else that happened then. Some days that TV show, watching Lindsay Scott, some days it seemed like that was the only good thing I had.*

Okay, I get it. Roz's voice was harsh now. *She's not nothing to you. Lindsay Scott saved your life. That's great. But—what you think of her? That's not real. She's not—what was her name on the show?*

Elizabeth Camplin.

Toby sounded reverent, so worshipful he could have been talking about Mother Teresa.

Elizabeth, then. That's not who she really is. Elizabeth Camplin's a made-up character. Some, I don't know, forty-five-year-old man with three ex-wives probably wrote all her lines. What you're obsessed with isn't even real. You don't know anything at all about Lindsay Scott herself.

I know she needs help. You said so yourself. She helped me when I needed it. What kind of person am I if I don't try to do everything I can to help her?

I gulped, surprised at the lump in my throat. I tried to send out a telepathic message of my own: *No, Toby, that's not the right conclusion. I don't need your help.* But my abilities were good only for receiving, not sending. My thoughts didn't travel.

Toby, you . . . I heard Roz say, and then I lost the thread of their conversation, lost it in an overwhelming wave of new voices:

Oh, look, there's that girl who . . .

I think this is the episode where Elizabeth loses her tooth.

Those old hairstyles are so funny. . . .

Hey! I used to have a sweater just like Lindsay Scott's!

Which one did you hate the most? Lindsay Scott, right?

It was eleven o'clock. Time for the next rerun of *Just Me and the Kids.*

I scrambled back to the doorstep. I couldn't listen anymore. Not unless I wanted to go crazy.

Chapter 9

I shoved my way in through the back door, my hands shaking. I slammed the door and collapsed against it, my trembling legs giving way. I slid all the way down to the floor, and wrapped my arms around my knees.

The silence engulfed me. Blessed silence, my sanctuary, my salvation, my sanity. It wasn't complete silence—I could hear the ticking of the clock on the living room wall. But all the voices were stilled.

Two times going outside in one night, I told myself. *The second time was even by choice. Wow, aren't you brave.*

I didn't know why my house was a silent zone, the one place where my secret skill disappeared. For all I knew, maybe there were hundreds of silent houses across the country, thousands or millions worldwide. Maybe there were even dead zones in some out-of-the-way places outdoors, like areas out of cell phone range. I hadn't experimented.

Maybe I was too scared of finding out that this tiny house was my only possible refuge?

I also didn't know how much my father had known.

When I was eleven, when I grew into my "talent," I had what probably looked like a nervous breakdown. *Kids* was canceled, in a sudden rain of bad reviews. I'm not sure how much of it was my fault. I played Elizabeth, the youngest child, who was supposed to be the overconfident know-it-all—the one who had all the answers the bumbling grown-ups were too stupid or harried to think of themselves. But suddenly I always looked terrorized and terrified. Suddenly I began stammering all my lines, freezing for no apparent reason, breaking down in the middle of a scene as if some invisible enemies had rushed in to stab me with a thousand invisible swords. I knew that the director and the other actors blamed me for ruining the show, that the network head used me as his excuse for pulling the plug.

I knew because I heard it all, all the mean things people said about me behind my back.

Please, just give us one more season. I know Lindsay's going through a bad spell, but—

Bad spell? She's atrocious! She looks like she's being tortured, just saying "That's so obvious."

That had been one of my trademark lines.

Well, you know, a lot of kids are thrown off-kilter when they hit puberty. Maybe we could write that into the character a little.

Yeah, a lot of kids get zits when they hit puberty too, but no one wants to see that on national TV.

Maybe if we just fire Lindsay? Or— I know! What if we plant some stories in the tabloids, that she's doing drugs, that she's sleeping with . . . who's the latest boy band hottie? That'll help the ratings!

I was eleven then. Eleven. And that suggestion was from Daniel DeLarue, the series director, who put his arm around me after one particularly horrible taping and told me that he loved me like his own daughter, that he never wanted anything bad to happen to me, that he'd always look out for me.

Was it any wonder that I stopped trusting anyone? That when the show ended I went into my bedroom, shut the door, and pretty much refused to come out? And this was in my old bedroom, in our old house in California, where I had no protection from the voices, the comments, the criticism, the cattiness. I just lay in bed with my pillow over my head and cried.

Most parents would have been worried. My father simply left trays of food and stacks of paperback books outside my bedroom door.

And then he announced that he had a new job and we were moving halfway across the country—no, more than halfway; got to get that geography right!—to Springdale, Illinois.

"It's where your mother's family was from," he said, as if I cared.

I put my hands over my ears every time he talked about

Springdale. I didn't help at all with the move. I was just another belonging my father had to transport two thousand miles, across eight states—only a little more flexible than a lamp, a little less rigid than the kitchen table.

I cowered in the hotel room bed while my father went out exploring Springdale, getting "the lay of the land," as he put it. I guessed he was house hunting, but I didn't listen to anything he said when he came back to the hotel each evening. There was too much other noise in my head; I *couldn't* listen. Then one morning he laid out clothes for me to wear, and he wouldn't give up, tugging me out of bed. Finally I understood that he was going to force me to look at our new house.

Stepping across the threshold that first time, feeling that first blast of silence . . . There are no words to describe how good that felt. Bliss, ecstasy, rapture—all inadequate words, pale imitations of the actual feeling. It was like starving and not knowing that food existed—and then being handed a gourmet meal. It was like drowning and being certain that you were about to die—and then unexpectedly, miraculously, being yanked from the water at the very last second. It was like being in prison and thinking you had a life sentence, no hope of ever getting out—and then being set free.

"Look okay to you?" my father asked as I stepped inside. He was ahead of me, holding the door.

I studied my father carefully, trying to read in his expression the meaning behind his words. Did he know? Had he picked this house on purpose? Had he possibly even arranged for its magical powers, requesting sound barriers the way some other home buyer might ask for a new coat of paint?

My father had a cheesy moustache, always in need of trimming. He wore his nondescript brownish hair in a comb-over. He had heavily rimmed glasses in a style that hadn't been fashionable since before *he* was born. Where Mrs. Mullin's glasses magnified her eyes, making her look more perceptive than she probably was, my father's glasses were more like a shield, something to hide behind. They seemed to cover most of his face.

I didn't have a clue what my father was thinking.

"Sure. Fine," I said, barely managing to hold back what could have been a ten-million-watt grin.

I should have told my father the truth. I know that. But you have to understand—I'd heard what my father said about me too.

Lindsay cares too much about her appearance. . . .

Lindsay doesn't understand transcendentalism the way I always thought any child of mine would. . . .

That TV show she's on is so stupid I can't even watch it. . . .

Well, yeah, of course I know she makes more money in a day than I make in a month. Isn't that a sign that society rewards all the wrong values? Aren't professors a thousand times more important than actors?

I walked through our house with pretend nonchalance.

"The kitchen's a little small, but I guess it will do," I said. And, "Are you sure we can fit a bed and a desk and a dresser in this bedroom?" And, "It looks kind of old. You don't think there are termites or anything like that, do you?"

And the whole time I was restraining the instinct to jump up and down and cheer and throw my arms around my father and scream, "Thank you! Thank you! You've saved my life!"

We moved into the house, and I think my father was proud of me then. I studied so hard I barely had time to leave the house. I guess I'm lucky that I had a father who thought it was a good thing that I sat at my computer all day, conjugating Spanish verbs, researching long-dead poets, solving convoluted physics problems. I'm lucky he wasn't the type of dad who would say, "That's enough computer time. Go out and get some fresh air." Or, "Don't you have any friends?"

Sitting with my back against the door, fresh from eavesdropping on Toby and Roz, I was surprised to discover that I had tears streaming down my face.

Hey, hey. Enough of that, I told myself. *Didn't you hear Roz say she wasn't going to go talk to Mrs. Mullin? You're safe.*

Safe.

Safe.

Safe.

Chapter 10

I couldn't sleep, so I finished my algebra homework.

Then, remembering the expression on Roz's face when she'd looked around my house, I dusted off the stacks of books in the living room.

For some reason that made me cry again.

I sank down into my father's reading chair and told myself a bedtime story: *Everything's going to turn out fine. You'll see. Tomorrow you can make all the arrangements for Operation: Get Rid of Mrs. Mullin. Once you take care of Mrs. Mullin, you'll feel a lot better.*

What I'd realized was that I needed Mrs. Mullin to leave me alone for only another year and a half, until I was eighteen. Thanks to a little computer research, I knew that Mrs. Mullin's husband, Elgin, was a retired archaeology professor who'd somehow never managed to achieve his dream of visiting the various archaeological sites of Greece and Turkey. This came out in old entries on a rate-your-professor site, where there'd actually been a debate between students who thought it was pathetic that he had so little experience and students who just felt sorry for him. But I could see how it must have happened. Springdale College had never paid well enough to finance such a trip, and Dr. Elgin Mullin had never distinguished himself quite enough to win any of the right kinds of grants.

I myself was lacking parents, friends, a chance to achieve my dreams, and, apparently, the ability to control my own tears. But, oh, I had money.

Except for a relatively modest "living allowance," all my earnings from *Just Me and the Kids* had gone into a trust fund. If I'd been a Lindsay Lohan or a Mary-Kate or Ashley Olsen, I could have blown through the living allowance very quickly. But spending five years sitting in front of a computer in Springdale, Illinois, is much, much cheaper than being a jet-setting ex-actress party girl in Los Angeles or New York.

I easily had enough money to give Elgin Mullin the grant he'd always wanted. There would be only three strings attached:

He had to take his wife.

He had to be away for at least a year and a half.

He'd have to leave as quickly as possible.

Brilliant, I told myself. *Genius.*

I still couldn't stop crying.

I curled up into a little ball, letting the tears soak into the arm of my father's chair. I don't know at what point I slipped over into sleep. But when I woke up again, my neck was stiff from lolling over the side of the chair at an odd angle. My eyes felt prickly from all the tears. My mouth was dry, a parched desert—when was the last time I'd had anything to eat or drink?

The sunlight streaming in the front window teased at my swollen eyelids. Sunlight, then shadow, then sunlight again.

Wow, I thought dazedly. *Those must be some really fast-moving clouds, blocking and then unblocking the sun so quickly.*

The clouds were apparently yelling, too, and making a tapping noise so close they could be right at my window.

I turned and stared straight out the glass, only inches from my face.

Toby and Roz were standing right there, just on the other side of the pane, knocking at the window and calling out, "Lindsay! Lindsay, are you okay?" It was Toby jumping up and down and waving his arms that kept blocking and unblocking the sun.

I gaped at them for a long moment, blinking my sore eyes once or twice in disbelief.

"Lindsay," Roz said, her mouth very close to the glass. "Open the door. Open the door and let us in or we'll call the police."

I wasn't so far gone that I couldn't see the absurdity of that—I'd been nice enough not to call the police when they'd kidnapped and trespassed, but they were threatening to report me for not letting them into my own house?

I sat up and reached over and jerked open the door just so I could tell them that. But as soon as the door moved, they burst in.

"Thank you. That was very good," Roz said, sounding like a teacher talking to a child with severe mental disabilities. "Now tell us. What did you take? What are you on?"

I had to blink a couple more times, to wait until the words made sense to me.

"N-n-nothing," I stammered.

"Are you sure?" Roz asked, edging her phone out of her blue jeans pocket. "I can still call the police."

She held up the phone like it was a weapon.

It is, I remembered. *If she calls the police, she'll tell them how old I am, and everyone will find out that Mrs. Mullin isn't really taking care of me and . . .*

"I'm sure," I said, trying to draw some firmness into my voice. "I was just sleeping. I . . . I was tired. I stayed up late last night."

"Doing what?" Roz asked, still in prosecuting attorney mode. She hadn't returned the phone to her pocket yet.

"*Algebra,*" I answered. "I'm a very serious student." *Yes,* I reminded myself. *You are.* This was like having a director explaining a role to me, explaining the motivation for the character I was supposed to be playing. "A lot of times I have to stay up late to finish all my work. I'm taking eight classes right now, and doubling up on the sciences so I can graduate early." This was working very well. I actually managed to glare a little at Toby. "I got behind last night when I was kidnapped."

"Sorry," Toby said, sounding appropriately abashed. "And sorry if we scared you. It's just . . . you looked like you were dead."

The way he was looking at me, his head tilted slightly to the side, his eyebrows raised in an almost puppy-doggish show of concern—it made me wonder what I looked like now. I had to glance down to remember what I was wearing: gray sweatpants that had once belonged to my dad, a red Springdale College T-shirt he'd gotten me for Christmas. It was the same thing I'd been wearing last night, the last time I'd seen Roz and Toby. But that was okay, wasn't it? Last night wasn't that long ago. They didn't have to know that I'd probably been wearing those same clothes for a week.

Apart from the clothes, well, my hair was so thick and wavy that it always looked like a horrible mess when I first woke up. I was sure it was sticking out in a hundred different directions. As for my face, I hadn't been wearing any makeup, so there wasn't any danger that it was smeared across my cheeks. But . . . *Oh, no. My eyes. Can Roz and Toby tell that my eyes are swollen? Do they know that I've been crying?*

Olivia Jerome, my old acting "sister," had had tons of advice for dealing with tear-swollen eyes. But most of her advice involved things such as cucumber slices and tea bags— things I didn't have time for right now.

Stop thinking about how you look, I told myself. *Act like you think you look great, and they'll think so too.*

It was the biggest trick of acting, the fact that it's all an illusion, and people are highly suggestible.

I stood up, to put myself on their level, and to begin herding them toward the door.

"Well, as you can see, I'm not dead," I told Toby, favoring him with the old Lindsay-Scott-the-actress publicity smile. An "appearances coach" had once spent hours working with me, getting me to recognize the exact width of smile that was most flattering to my face. I hoped the calculation still applied now that my face was five years older.

Toby took a step back.

Oh, yeah, I thought mockingly. *I'm so devastatingly beautiful.*

Even Roz relaxed the hand holding her phone.

"You can understand why we were worried, can't you?" she asked.

I was saved from having to answer that because a dog began to bark excitedly out front.

Toby and Roz exchanged glances.

"I almost forgot," Roz said. She looked back at me, an odd look on her face. "I was feeling bad for you, about your dad and all—"

"I'm sorry," Toby interrupted in a rush. "Darnell and I didn't know, and we probably made things worse with what we did, and—"

"Don't worry about it," I said, holding up my hand to stop him, like a magnanimous queen pardoning a petty criminal. Considering I'd been awake for only about five minutes, I thought my acting was masterful.

"Anyhow, I was thinking about what would cheer me up if I were you, and, I don't know, maybe this is silly, but I thought if you just met my dog, maybe it would make you feel a little bit better," Roz said. She sounded uncertain now, like she'd just realized that she might be intruding. "Tina, this other waitress at Straley's, she finally dumped her no-good boyfriend, but she was really upset about it, and she said just looking into Barkley's eyes made a world of difference."

"Barkley's the dog," Toby contributed.

"Stupid name, right?" Roz asked. "Way too obvious. But my stepsister named him, and she's only eight, and she thought it was brilliant."

During this barrage of talk, Roz was easing her arm through the crook of my elbow and tugging me toward the door.

I was still digesting this turn of events. First I thought, *See, I knew Roz had to have a puppy, the way she talked about Toby and Darnell.* Then I realized, *They want me to go outside again? Just to look at a dog?* By the time my brain reached *Oh, no. You have got to be kidding!* Roz had already pulled me over to the doorway.

I stiffened and dug in my heels.

"I'm not much of a dog person," I said. "I'll just look out from here."

"Oh, everyone's a dog person around Barkley," Roz said lightly. Too lightly. There was something else hiding in her voice, some suspicion, some ulterior motive.

She's testing me, I thought. *She wants to see how I react.*

I had a pair of flip-flops by the front door. I couldn't quite recall if they'd fallen off my feet in the night, when I was huddled in my father's chair, or if they'd fallen there some other night, some other time when I'd been crying. But I slipped them on now, twisting my feet almost backward to scoop them up, to compensate for the odd way the flip-flops had landed. By then Toby had the door pulled wide open, and a burst of fresh air blew in, the strong spring wind tossing my hair about, creating instant tangles. I balanced my feet on the threshold, on that little ridge of wood that separated indoors from outdoors.

Roz was watching me very carefully.

I held my hair out of my face with one hand, and stepped down onto the doorstep very casually, very nonchalantly, as if there were no difference whatsoever between the house, the threshold, and the step.

There wasn't.

I don't know why, but my house's protection—my house's blessed silence—extends about a foot out from its walls in every direction. I've speculated that it's like radio signals, or radio-jamming signals, or cell phone jamming signals, or some other mysterious electronic phenomenon I don't really understand. I've never found anything that looks like a transmitter anywhere in the house, but I have to admit, I don't actually know what I'm looking for. I'm just glad that my chatter-free zone extends far enough that I can breathe fresh air in peace every now and then. Like I was doing the night before, when Toby and Darnell grabbed me.

I looked back at Roz in triumph. Something had changed in her face, a bafflement creeping over her expression that she wasn't quick enough to hide.

You're just not as good an actress as I am, are you? I almost taunted her.

The breeze had completely awakened me now. I was very alert. I thought I even knew what she was testing.

I bet she thought I was agoraphobic, given how I behaved last night. She thought I was one of those people who are afraid to go outdoors, and that's why I didn't escape from the Party Barn when I had the chance. Sorry, Roz, you are wrong! *You don't understand me at all!*

"Come on," Roz said, tugging on my elbow again, trying to pull me down off the step to the sidewalk.

Oh. Oh, no.

Standing on the doorstep wasn't proof enough for Roz. She'd still be suspicious unless I walked on out to the curb, where Roz's car was parked and a dog was tied to the car's door handle. The dog was barking incessantly and straining at his leash, constantly trying to launch himself out into the grass before being jerked back by his collar, again and again and again.

I pulled back, pressing my back against the wall of my house.

"What time is it?" I asked Roz. "I mean"—I covered quickly—"why aren't you and Toby in school?"

Roz lifted her cell phone again, checking the time.

"It's one thirty. In the afternoon," she said. "As my mom would say, you've slept half the day away."

"And we're done with school for the day," Toby said, grinning. "Roz and I both get early release, because of our jobs. But we both called in to work and said we'd be late. So we could check on you."

One thirty, I thought. *One thirty.*

One thirty was fairly safe, because it wasn't a likely time for *Just Me and the Kids* reruns. Or, if they were on, it was probably only preschoolers and stay-at-home moms watching them, and I could usually ignore their comments pretty easily. Sometimes, when my dad was still alive, one thirty was even a time when I'd chosen to go out, on purpose, for some unavoidable errand. Buying shoes, for example. I just had to be back by three.

Three was when the *Just Me and the Kids* reruns came on at a lot of prisons.

It's not going to take an hour and a half to walk out there, pat the dog's head a time or two, and send Toby and Roz away, I assured myself.

I shoved away from the wall and stepped down from the doorstep.

And then I froze, because I'd stepped down right into the middle of a conversation:

. . . had a daughter, didn't he?

Yeah, real mousy thing, always looked like she might die of fright if somebody actually spoke to her.

Why is it that people who have no social skills don't try to keep their kids from having the same problems?

What, you mean, like, they should sign their kids up for remedial socialization tutoring?

Yeah, can't you see it? Maybe there'd be field trips to normal life. "Now, boys and girls, we're going to prepare by working on a really hard lesson. When someone says hello to you, you say 'hello' back. Can you all repeat after me? Hel-lo!"

This was said in an overly prissy Mr. Rogers–like voice, followed by mocking laughter.

Yeah, well, Curran wasn't smart enough to figure that out. He was actually homeschooling his daughter.

You're kidding. Wasn't she weird enough already?

More laughter.

I thought I knew who was talking: two snarky grad assistants who'd shown up at my father's funeral. One had snorted with laughter when the funeral director mispronounced my father's name. The other had smirked when he'd muttered "Hey, sorry your dad's dead" beside the coffin.

They're the ones who need lessons in remedial social skills, I fumed. *Don't they know you're not supposed to speak ill of the dead?*

For a second I had a kind of fantasy in my head of stalking over to the college campus, bursting into the English department, hunting up those idiot grad assistants, and shouting at them, "For your information, I was *cultivating* that mousy image! I was cultivating it so I wouldn't have to hear fools like you talking about me. You weren't *supposed* to notice me. And next time you go to a funeral, show some respect now, you hear?"

It was almost fun to imagine how stunned they'd look: their eyes bugging out, their jaws dropping, their pretentious English-grad-student glasses slipping down their noses.

Toby touched my arm. "Lindsay?" he said gently. "Are you all right?"

I shook my head to clear it, my little fantasy vanishing. Of course I couldn't do any of that. Not without revealing too much. I couldn't ever risk letting anyone like those awful grad assistants know how weird I really was.

Unfortunately, the voices remained—the grad assistants'; a toddler's screaming at her mother, *No want nap! Want see Liz-Bet! Want see Liz-Bet!*; a casting director somewhere in Hollywood saying *She has that same wise-beyond-her-years quality as a young Lindsay Scott,* and his assistant reminding him, *But look what happened to her. . . .*

I forced myself to focus my eyes on Toby's face. His eyes—dark blue, I saw now, an unusual color with his brown hair—were kind and worried.

"I'm fine," I lied.

I concentrated on walking out to the curb, to the frantic dog exhausting himself trying to escape.

"Down, boy," Roz said behind me. "Down. Sit."

The dog whimpered but dropped its rear to the ground. I patted his head gingerly, drawing on my best acting skills.

"He's such a pretty color," I said, even managing to paste an admiring look onto my face.

"That's the golden retriever in him," Roz said eagerly. "We think his mother was part collie, part Lab, but his dad was golden retriever—well, not that he wasn't a mutt too, but he was *mostly* golden retriever."

I didn't know what to say to that. Dog studies hadn't been in my curriculum in the past five years, and the dogs we'd had on the show had been off-limits except when the cameras were rolling. And it was hard to focus on the dog with all that background noise in my head.

"Of course, you're probably used to purebred dogs," Roz went on, filling the gap in the conversation. Or—I squinted at her—maybe she wasn't just making conversation. Maybe she was insecure, thinking I was such a snob I'd think her dog was inadequate.

"I've never had a dog," I said stiffly.

To prove that I wasn't agoraphobic, that I wasn't a snob, that I didn't lack social skills, I crouched down and scratched Barkley behind the ears. And, from that angle, I couldn't see the Buick Regal pulling up behind Roz's car. Because of the noise in my head, and the dog breathing in my ear, I didn't really notice the sound of the car engine shutting off, the car door opening and closing.

So my first hint that I was truly in trouble was when I looked up and saw a woman in a turquoise polyester dress standing beside Roz and Toby, the sunshine glinting off her thick glasses.

It was Mrs. Mullin.

Chapter 11

"Hello, Lindsay," Mrs. Mullin said. "It's nice to see you're out getting some fresh air on this lovely day."

Was it just my imagination, or had she put a little too much emphasis on that one word, "out"? And what did that mysterious half smile mean?

I made a noise that probably sounded more like choking than actual speech.

"I don't believe I've met your friends," she said.

"Roz Tanner," Roz said, wiping off a bit of dog slobber on her pants and then offering her hand to Mrs. Mullin to shake. "Nice to meet you."

"Toby Dean," Toby said, following suit.

Neither of them pointed out that they weren't really my friends.

"And I'm Inez Mullin," Mrs. Mullin said. She leaned down slightly and scratched Barkley's right ear. "Who's this adorable fellow?"

"Oh!" Roz said, sounding startled, as if she'd forgotten about the dog. "His name's Barkley."

Had Roz just figured out that this wasn't just some random old lady wandering Springdale's streets? Did she know this was the person Toby had tried to get her to intervene with on my behalf?

Roz glanced over at Toby and jerked her head in Mrs. Mullin's direction. Yes. Roz knew.

Mrs. Mullin was still bent over Barkley, and didn't see.

"Is he full grown yet?" I asked desperately. "Barkley, I mean—is he going to get any bigger?"

"Well, he's going to have to grow into those paws," Mrs. Mullin said, in that indulgent, cutesy voice that people use to talk to animals and babies. "Look at the size of those feet."

I gasped, and murmured "Wow, they're huge!"—as if I'd just come across Bigfoot himself. Really, they just looked like dogs' feet to me, but the longer we spent talking about Barkley, the longer I could keep Roz and Toby and Mrs. Mullin away from other topics.

Mrs. Mullin's eyes seemed to see through me from behind her glasses.

"Lindsay, I just wanted to stop in quickly on my lunch break to give you your dad's mail," she said. "I thought you might want to look at it now, rather than later in the day." Somehow her voice had turned solemn now, respectful even of a dead man's mail. The snarky grad students could take lessons in respect from her. "But I don't want to interrupt you and your friends. I'll just put this on your counter, all right?"

She held up a couple of letters—probably all academic junk mail, and renewal notices for obscure journals like *Transcendentalist Times*. My father's death had undoubtedly cut their subscription rolls in half.

To my surprise Mrs. Mullin didn't linger to wait for my answer. She trotted—rather spryly—up the sidewalk and into my house.

"Uh," I said. I wanted to protest, to keep her from violating my sanctuary. Every other time she'd stopped by, I'd stood on the doorstep, keeping her out. But I couldn't make a big deal about it now, because then Toby and Roz would figure out that she was nothing to me, that I'd never even met her before my father's funeral.

"She seems nice," Roz said. "You say she and your father were—"

At the last minute I remembered what I'd strongly implied before.

"Friends," I said firmly. "Very, very close friends."

"Right," Roz said, sounding relieved.

Even if I had wanted to make Roz and Toby believe that my father had been quite old when I was born—and therefore make them believe that he and Mrs. Mullin had been contemporaries and potential lovers—it just didn't seem possible, with Mrs. Mullin right there, to think of her having an affair. She wouldn't cheat on her husband. She'd probably been married since time began. She probably cooked dinner for her husband every night, even though he was retired and she wasn't. She probably did his laundry and ironed his sheets and sewed buttons on his shirts, like a grandma in a sitcom TV show. That was the type of woman she looked like.

She came back.

"Well, it's back to the salt mines for me," she said.

She reached out and touched a strand of my hair that had escaped from my grasp. Then she tucked it carefully behind my ear, with all the rest. It was a grandmotherly gesture, a motherly gesture, something much too intimate for a random old lady I barely knew. It was all I could do not to flinch.

She turned back to Toby and Roz.

"Take care of Lindsay, okay?" she instructed them. "She's been through a tough time lately, as I'm sure you know. She can use all the friends she can get."

"Okay," Roz promised, sounding as stunned as I felt.

Then Mrs. Mullin walked past us and slipped back into her car.

None of us said anything as we watched her drive away, hunched over her huge steering wheel. Questions were exploding in my mind like fireworks: *What was that all about? What's she trying to do? Why was she smiling like Mona Lisa the whole time? Did she say or do anything that would ruin the story I told Roz?*

I mentally reviewed every word, every gesture, every gleam of Mrs. Mullin's bespectacled eyes. I began to relax, even absentmindedly patting Barkley's head again. It was uncanny. Mrs. Mullin certainly had not come out and said,

"I've all but moved in with Lindsay, to make sure she's all right. I'm taking very good care of her." But she might as well have. It was almost like she'd known exactly what I'd needed her to say and do.

But how could she have?

Roz's cell phone rang, blaring out—surprisingly—a snatch of classical music I should have recognized but didn't. It was full of yearning violins. She flipped the phone open and lifted it to her ear.

"Yeah, he's with me," I heard her say. "Okay. Okay. Soon as we can."

She shut the phone.

"Darnell?" Toby asked.

"Yeah. He says you've got three washers and two dryers to deliver and install before five o'clock, and one of those deliveries is way down in Straitersburg."

"Okay," Toby said.

He looked toward me and—I don't know. I was an actress all those years, right? I heard people talking all the time about how to hide what you're really feeling, how to make it look like you're in the grip of some profound emotion you've maybe never even felt in your entire life. "Talent" was being able to look like you were desperately in love or deeply in despair or overwhelmingly happy or *something*—when, really, you were just wondering what was for lunch.

Toby's expression was the opposite of all that. His face was full of naked emotion, longing and regret—unadorned, unhidden. Genuine.

I had to look away.

"We have to go," Roz said, starting to unfasten Barkley's leash.

"You'll be all right?" Toby asked me. That sincerity . . . He could go to Hollywood, get his teeth capped, maybe have the little scar by his eye fixed, and then make millions playing kind but dumb backwoods hottie roles. They'd even want him in the very same flannel-shirt-over-long-johns-with-well-worn-jeans outfit he was wearing now.

Of course, if he went to Hollywood, got his teeth capped, and had his scar fixed, he probably wouldn't stay sincere.

"I'm fine," I said, shrugging. I wasn't. I was feeling unaccountably sad at the thought of Toby Dean going to Hollywood.

"Well . . . ," Roz said, watching me. "We just wanted to make sure."

I reminded myself that expressing genuine emotion wasn't permissible for someone like me. I snapped back into acting mode.

"Thanks, I guess," I said. I forced myself to grin. "Good luck with all those washers and dryers, Toby."

"Maybe we'll come back and check on you some other time?" Toby asked wistfully.

"Sure," I said, shrugging. It was an old acting trick, saying a word to make it sound like I meant the exact opposite. My "Sure" was hostile, a keep-out sign, a clear warning: *No, I do not want you to come back, buddy. Leave me alone!*

But what if what I really wanted to say was "Sure"?

Chapter 12

I sat down on my doorstep after Toby and Roz left. I leaned forward a little, telling myself I needed to hear what they said about me, just in case. For that matter I needed to hear if Mrs. Mullin said anything about me or my dad or my living arrangements when she got back to the English department at Springdale College.

I wasn't used to *trying* to listen. I'd spent the past five years of my life trying desperately to block out every utterance I was so unnaturally capable of overhearing. Even the admiring comments—*Lindsay Scott is my favorite actress! . . . Ooh, I love the way she says "That's so obvious!" . . . Can I get my hair cut like Lindsay Scott's?*—became cloying when I heard them again and again and again. One time a bunch of eight-year-olds at a sleepover in Oklahoma woke me up in the middle of the night in California because they were screaming, *We love you, Lindsay! We love you, Lindsay!* at the top of their lungs. And, of course, I heard it. Another time, I had to get up and leave in the middle of a math test my on-set tutor was giving me—I had to pretend I was sick—because a mall in Texas was having a Lindsay Scott look-alike contest. So, instead of math, my head was full of, *Oh, I wish I was as pretty as Lindsay. . . . You've got eyes just like Lindsay's. . . . Lindsay's walk isn't quite that prancy. Try that again. . . .* Some of the other actors and actresses on *Just Me and the Kids* used to complain about how autograph-seekers would interrupt them when they were out shopping or eating. A lot of that, I thought, was actually bragging. ("I got interrupted seven times during dinner last night." "That's nothing, I got interrupted twelve times—and I was eating fast food!") But before we moved to Springdale, I felt like I had all the autograph-seekers in my head, all the time.

It was worse when I started having problems on the set of *Just Me and the Kids.* The *I want to look like Lindsay* and the *Ooh, I love her!* comments began to feel mocking, as cruel as the criticism.

How could anyone possibly have liked me?

So I sat on the step for a few moments, steadying myself, before dipping my head forward. Silence . . . silence . . . NOISE!

. . . and this one time I met the whole cast of Just Me and the Kids *and the little kid—what was her name? Lindsay something—she . . .*

Liz-Bet's funny!

Yes, honey, she . . .

We handle trust funds for several child stars, including . . .

It was harder than I would have thought to pull Roz's and Toby's voices out of the cacophony. I'd done it the night before, but they'd been talking loudly then, almost arguing at some points. This time their voices were soft, muted.

Huh, I thought. *Volume matters.*

Then I did the mental equivalent of pricking up my ears, leaning closer, listening hard.

I know, I know, Toby was saying. *You're going to tell me she's none of my business and I need to butt out.*

Yeah . . . Roz's voice sounded vague, uncertain. *That's probably true. That old lady looked like she had everything under control.*

I smiled. That was just what I wanted her to think.

Toby didn't answer right away, and for a moment I thought I'd lost the conversation. Maybe that was all they had to say about me?

Then I heard Toby's voice again, very soft. *She did look dead. Even awake she still looked . . . out of it.*

Traumatized, Roz agreed. *Her dad just died. What do you expect? Do you want to know what you looked like every day of seventh grade?*

I remember. But I . . .

His voice faded away. I waited. It didn't come back.

No! Wait! I wanted to scream. *I wasn't done listening yet!* I strained my ears, my mental ears, as I never had before. I leaned so far forward I practically fell off the step. But it was like standing at the back of a huge room packed with noisy screaming people and trying to eavesdrop on two people whispering at the front.

I couldn't hear Roz or Toby. But I heard another familiar voice: Mrs. Mullin's.

That's Lindsay, last name Curran. Or Scott. . . . Uh-huh. The father's name was Arthur Scott Curran. . . . Yes, I'd appreciate it if you'd check.

Chapter 13

I jumped up from my doorstep, an automatic response. I jerked my head around, right to left, left to right, searching frantically, as if I thought I'd be able to see Mrs. Mullin and whoever she was talking to. I ran out to the curb, to peer down the street toward the college. If any of my neighbors were watching, they'd undoubtedly think I looked crazy, maybe like a homeless person with the d.t.'s, sparring with invisible demons.

I couldn't see anything. I couldn't hear Mrs. Mullin's voice anymore. I'd never heard anything from the person she'd been talking to.

Why not? I wondered. *If Mrs. Mullin was talking about me, wasn't the other person talking about me too? So shouldn't I have heard that? Aren't those the rules?*

The wind whipped my hair into my face once more, and I shivered, suddenly chilled. I'd never had reason before to doubt my talent. Disparage it, yes, bemoan it, curse it, even—but it had never *abandoned* me like that.

Isn't that what you want? A tiny voice—my own—whispered in my head.

Not now! I ranted to myself. *Not when I need to know what Mrs. Mullin is up to!*

I mentally played back the exact words I'd heard. She'd said, *Uh-huh.* She'd said, *Yes, I'd appreciate it if you'd check.* She'd certainly sounded like she was talking back and forth with somebody else. Who?

Even though I couldn't see anything out of the ordinary, I stood by the curb for a long time, gazing toward the slate roof of the Springdale College English department four blocks away. A group of giggly girls in sorority sweatshirts passed by, and a few minutes later, I "heard" them say, *That girl really needed a makeover!* And then, *Do you think she even owns a hairbrush?* And, *Or shampoo?* They giggled harder. I could still see them, two blocks away, passing under the bare-limbed poplars at the edge of the campus. Their shoulders shook with the laughter. So that was proof, in real time, that my "talent" was working. I just couldn't hear anything else from Toby or Roz or Mrs. Mullin, or anything at all from Mrs. Mullin's conversation partner.

Maybe I should go confront Mrs. Mullin? Tell her thanks for bringing Dad's mail, thanks for his paycheck and the casserole and everything else, but, really, like Greta Garbo, I just want to be left alone.

I wouldn't be able to carry it off. I hadn't been able to say that within the silence and protection of my own house. I certainly wouldn't be able to say it in the middle of the English department office, with people passing by, with who knew what voices calling out in my head. Certainly not with the three o'clock reruns approaching.

I glanced up at the Springdale College clock tower. The hour hand was already on the three, the minute hand closing in on twelve.

"Oooh . . . ," I moaned. I looked back and forth—the clock, my house, the clock, my house—before finally, at the last second, scrambling back toward my doorstep.

I stood there for a moment, panting, aggravated. I didn't know who Mrs. Mullin had been talking to, or what the other person planned to check. I couldn't know, not without eavesdropping endlessly or just coming right out and asking Mrs. Mullin. Neither of those things was going to happen. So that left—what?

Operation: Get Rid of Mrs. Mullin, I reminded myself.

The plan didn't seem as brilliant and shiny and perfect as it had before. For one thing, what if whatever Mrs. Mullin had just set in motion had already gone too far before she and Mr. Mullin headed off to Turkey?

You'll just have to hurry, I told myself grimly.

I went back inside, sat down at my computer, and forced myself to begin typing:

Dear Mr. Mullin:

I reminded myself he had his doctorate, and would need to be flattered.

Dear Dr. Mullin:
We at the

I needed a good name, credible-sounding but anonymous, something that Dr. Mullin would think he might have heard of, even if it wasn't real.

Dear Dr. Mullin:
We at the Smith Foundation award a small number of grants to professors emeriti who have distinguished themselves in their field over the course of their entire career . . .

I was off. From there the words flowed smoothly out of my fingertips. It was almost as if I believed that Dr. Mullin truly had been an extraordinary professor, an influence on hundreds of lives. I had no idea what kind of professor Dr. Mullin was for real, but I praised his scholarship, his dedication, his teaching style, his contributions to the field. I made up anonymous alumni who'd supposedly cared enough to nominate Dr. Mullin for this great honor: eighteen months abroad, all expenses paid. I Googled a couple of archaeology sites, and dropped in a paragraph or two about the glories of life on an archaeological dig.

It was a masterpiece.

I sat back, rereading the words on the screen, admiring my work. All I had to do now was design some fancy stationery, maybe with a fake crest for the fake Smith Foundation. A fake Latin motto would be a nice touch too. Then I'd just drop the letter in the mail . . .

The mail.

In a horrid burst of insight, I saw the flaw in my perfect plan. If I stuck my alleged Smith Foundation letter into the mailbox on the front of my house—or even if I walked it down to the post office five blocks away—it would arrive at the Mullins' house with a Springdale postmark.

Maybe the Mullins wouldn't notice. But if they did, they'd know the Smith Foundation was fake. Springdale was a small town; if an educational foundation existed anywhere within its borders, everyone at Springdale College would know.

I couldn't mail my letter from Springdale.

I thought about mailing the letter in a separate envelope to someone I knew back in California, and asking him or her to take the letter out and remail it, getting that precious Los Angeles postmark. The only problem with that was, unless you counted the people managing my finances (and I didn't), there wasn't anyone I'd stayed in touch with from California. There wasn't anyone anywhere I'd stayed in touch with, not enough to ask a favor like that.

I clenched my fists, banged them against my desk. I glared out the window, and my gaze fell on my father's car, which was parked on the side street, looking abandoned and forlorn. Someone from the English department had kindly brought it home the day my father died. Whoever it was had dropped the keys directly into my hand, all the time mumbling condolences. I couldn't summon a face or a name to attach to that deed, couldn't even remember if it'd been a man or a woman. I'd been too staggered to pay attention.

But I had a car! Why hadn't I ever bothered to learn how to drive? I could have practiced in the middle of the night. It would have required driving around Springdale's dark streets with clenched teeth, my father at my side. He probably would have assumed that my tension was only because I feared hitting a parked car, feared not being able to react in time if a cat ran out into the street.

Tears swam in my eyes because my father and I had missed that sitcom moment, the dad teaching his daughter to drive.

So what? We missed everything together, I told myself, angrily brushing the tears away. What mattered now was that I *didn't* know how to drive. I could see how simple it would have been: If I could drive, I could hop in Dad's car— so casually! so easily!—and I could drive to . . . Oh, Chicago was big enough, wasn't it? The chatter in my head wouldn't be so bad if I went, say, at three in the morning. I could stick my letter in any one of dozens of mailboxes for that precious Chicago postmark. Hundreds, even. And then—the possibilities fell into place—I could cement my deception by also buying a cell phone that would have a Chicago area code, so I could provide a phone number for Dr. Mullin to call for verification and further arrangements. I'd been planning to just set up a website for the Smith Foundation, and had included a paragraph about how all communication about the grant would henceforth be online. But a phone number would be so much better, sound so much less suspicious. Of course that would require revising the letter to provide the new number, but if I could drive, I could do that at an all-night copy shop, somewhere near the phone store and the mailbox. Everything was possible if I could drive.

But I couldn't.

I slumped over my computer. My mind, traitorously, provided me with an image from my acting days: the car service coming to pick me up every morning to take me to the set. All those long black cars . . . That would have worked for me now, too, in the absence of my own driving knowledge. But Springdale didn't have a car service. It was such a small town, it didn't even have a taxi company. Toby and Darnell, delivering their washers and dryers and couches, were probably the closest thing to a taxi company within a fifty-mile radius.

I jerked upright again. *Delivering. Deliverance.* Wasn't that exactly what I wanted? I laughed, giddy. My solution was so clear. Hadn't Toby and Darnell already offered to take me anywhere I wanted to go?

Chapter 14

I forced myself to slow down, think everything through.
This was like a tricky algebra problem: I didn't want to skip
any steps in the beginning that would get me in trouble later
on. I even went downstairs and fixed myself a peanut butter
and jelly sandwich, on the theory that I'd think better with
some food in my stomach. The bread was dry and stale, dating back to some grocery trip my father had made before
he died. My father's penchant for buying cheap preservative-
laden bread was the only thing that saved me from eating
mold.

I still threw the sandwich away after the first bite. It didn't
even taste like food.

I did feel fortified enough to get back on the computer
and find, on Google Earth, the location of post offices, late-
night copy shops, and possible places to buy cell phones in

the Chicago area. I thought it'd be too hard finding a cell phone provider that was open past nine or ten, but I'd underestimated the night-owl habits of college students. Near the University of Chicago, I had my choice of three different stores that sold cell phones and were open twenty-four hours a day.

Perfect.

I didn't have a phone number for Toby or Darnell, but I remembered they were delivering washers and dryers in Straitersburg, which—thank you, again, Google Earth—was evidently a truly tiny town about a half an hour south of Springdale. I found a Straitersburg Appliance Store and took a chance and called.

"Hello. I'm trying to get in touch with someone who does delivery work for you—a Toby Dean?" I asked, trying to sound older. I pictured myself in the role of a forty-something housewife who considered the arrival of her new washer the most exciting moment of her life. There'd been a lot of women like that in the commercials that ran during *Just Me and the Kids*.

"Hold on. He just walked in," the voice on the other end of the line said. The next words were muffled, as if the woman on the phone had covered the receiver with her hand. Still, I heard them well enough: "Toby, honey, this call's for you. You finally got yourself a girlfriend?"

I blushed. I guessed I hadn't sounded like a fortysomething housewife.

I heard Toby say, at a distance, "It's probably just Roz," and then, directly into the phone, "Hello?"

I was suddenly tongue-tied. It was that word, "girlfriend," that did it. I gulped.

"Um, hi, Toby. This is Lindsay. I, uh, had a favor to ask."

"Lindsay," he said, with a quickening interest in his voice that made my heart beat a little faster. "What do you need?"

I hesitated.

"I need to have something delivered. Well, actually, it's sort of . . . me. I need someone to drive me to Chicago."

"You're leaving?" Toby said, and there was something in his voice I couldn't quite decipher over the phone. Was he going to lecture me about not becoming a runaway?

"*No.* I just need to . . . drop something off. And pick something up. Run a few errands," I said. This didn't seem convincing enough. "I'm putting together a surprise for Mrs. Mullin, to thank her for everything she's done for me."

Toby let out a deep breath. It almost sounded like a sigh of relief.

"Well, that's nice," he said. "For a minute there, the way you were talking about 'errands,' I was afraid you were dealing drugs or something."

The words were teasing, but I heard the question in them.

"Oh, believe me, this isn't anything illegal," I said. "Or immoral. It's a gift."

And it was, I reminded myself. I was going to be giving the Mullins lots and lots of money. I was going to make them very happy.

It was going to help me, too, but Toby didn't need to know that.

"And I'll pay you," I promised. "Double your usual rate, whatever that is."

"Oh, you don't need to do that," he said. "I think Darnell and me still owe you, after what happened last night. Or—" He seemed to be reconsidering. "How about if you just pay the gas money?"

"Deal," I said. "And you can use my dad's car. Not put so many miles on yours."

"Okay," Toby said. "Want me to ask Darnell when we're available? And . . . maybe see if Roz wants to come too? She's always talking about how much she loved it, the one time she went to Chicago."

"No!" I said quickly. I could just picture it, Roz and Toby and Darnell and me, all trapped in a car for four hours, round-trip. Roz was too inquisitive, too combative. It'd be too much for me, fending off her questions for so long, the whole time trying to think over the buzzing in my head. I'd let something slip, make a mistake. I couldn't risk it.

And Darnell . . . I didn't think he was that much less gullible than Toby. But he was one more person to see holes in my story, to think up questions I couldn't or wouldn't want to answer.

"How about if it's just you and me?" I said. "I actually need to do this in a big hurry. Any chance you could meet me at midnight?"

Toby was quiet for a minute, and I was certain he was about to say no. *He's suspicious; he doesn't trust me.*

"All right," Toby said. "See you then."

I hung up. I'd done it! I'd arranged everything! I waited for the triumphant glee to wash over me, the euphoria of accomplishment.

Instead I felt flat. Deflated. Scared.

Except for my bizarre trip to the Party Barn the night before, I hadn't been more than six blocks away from my house's protection in five years. Chicago was a hundred and twenty miles away. Even during my father's funeral, I hadn't spent more than two hours outside my house's silence. And now I'd just arranged to be away—far away—for probably five hours, by the time I took care of everything. How could I do this?

How could I not?

Chapter 15

Toby came early.

I saw him pull around the corner in a pick-up truck at 11:50, so I had to beckon him into the house on the pretense of still needing to get my things together. There was no way I was starting this trip before the eleven o'clock reruns were over.

Toby stepped into the living room, with a look on his face like he thought he was trespassing.

"I just need to run upstairs for a minute," I said. "Do you want something to drink while you're waiting?" I was proud of myself for thinking to ask that. It sounded very . . . normal. "We've got, uh . . ." I remembered the last of the milk had gone sour a week ago. I'd drunk the last of the orange juice. I crossed into the kitchen and opened the door of the space that Dad and I had always called the pantry—an overly grand name for the tiny closet. "Let's see. Sam's Choice cola?"

"Someone like you drinks Wal-Mart brand?" Toby asked.

I didn't, not really. The cola was from a twelve-pack Dad had bought for some English faculty potluck. Evidently no one drank Sam's Choice cola, which was why it was still in our pantry.

I just shrugged at Toby.

"Sometimes," I said.

"Thanks," he said, coming up behind me to reach into the pack for a can.

Toby was now between me and the stairs, the kitchen table blocking my path on the other side. I didn't know how to get past him without it being weird.

"Um," I said.

"Oh, sorry," Toby said, stepping back against the wall. He cradled his soda can in his hands like it was something precious.

I shoved past the pantry door, shoving a little too hard, perhaps. It slammed shut. I flinched, overreacting. Then I felt like I had to explain my jumpiness.

"Mrs. Mullin is asleep upstairs," I said. "She's been staying over a lot of nights, so I'm not alone. So we have to be quiet."

Now, why did I pick that explanation? Panic swept over Toby's face. He instantly froze, as if taking a breath might make too much noise.

"But don't worry too much," I said, trying to backpedal. "She's a pretty sound sleeper."

Toby still looked horrified.

"She doesn't know you're going to Chicago, does she?" he asked, his voice hoarse with anxiety. "Are you sure . . . I mean, what if she wakes up in the middle of the night and peeks in on you, just to make sure everything's okay?"

Did adults do that for sixteen-year-old kids? For a second I let myself imagine what that would be like. To my knowledge, my father had never checked on me in the middle of the night, even when I was little. But I still found myself nearly knocked down with a wave of missing him, practically a physical pain that made it hard to keep standing.

"I'm leaving a note on my bed for Mrs. Mullin," I said, my voice coming out oddly even and calm. Robotic. "Just in case. But I'm sure she won't wake up."

"Oh," Toby said. "That's a good idea."

I wasn't sure he was convinced, but at least he wasn't stalking out, refusing to drive me, refusing to take part in my subterfuge, even if it was for a gift for Mrs. Mullin.

"I'll be really fast," I said, before he had a chance to change his mind.

I made a show of tiptoeing up the stairs, grinning the whole time to show that my stealth was well-intentioned, that I knew Mrs. Mullin would forgive me all my sneaking around when she finally got her gift. I hesitated in my room for about as long as it would have taken me to scrawl a quick note. Then I grabbed my purse and did the same exaggerated tiptoeing act back down the stairs. I'd already stuffed my purse with everything I needed: the directions I'd printed out from the Internet, my flash drive with the draft of my letter to Mr. Mullin, my MasterCard, and a wad of cash just in case someone balked at taking a charge card from a teenager. (That had happened in one of the *Just Me and the Kids* episodes, leading to my "big sister" picketing the store. I wouldn't be doing that.) Earlier that night I'd also showered and actually spent time on my hair and makeup—more time than I'd spent in probably five years. It seemed important to try to look as old as possible, but I couldn't decide if I looked older with my hair pulled back or hanging straight down. I'd fooled around with it for an hour, finally giving up and leaving it down simply out of frustration. It'd grown a lot in the past five years. I couldn't remember the last time I'd actually bothered letting Dad cut it, or cut it myself. Did *that* make me look older—dour, maybe, like a teenage wife in one of those religious sects that don't believe in letting women cut their hair?

Possibly, I told myself, catching a glimpse of my reflection in the glass on one of Dad's framed prints. My clothes were nondescript enough to go along with that character. I had on khaki pants and a plain blue button-up shirt: it was my costume from any time my dad had any of his fellow adjunct faculty buddies drop by. The clothes very distinctly said, *Don't notice me. Forget I'm even here.* I didn't actually have any clothes that were more interesting than that. Five years ago I'd had someone dressing me, scouring stores for just the right look for Lindsay Scott. When I lost that, I'd done nothing to learn anything about fashion or hair or makeup myself.

So? I asked myself. *You're just going to mail a letter.*

"Ready?" Toby said. He was standing in the living room now, still holding the unopened can of soda cupped in his hands. Maybe he thought popping the top would be too noisy.

I glanced at the clock on the wall. Both hands pointed straight up.

"Sure," I said.

Toby stepped out into the darkness ahead of me. I turned out the living room light and locked the door. I braced myself to step down into the chatter, but it wasn't too bad. Most of what I heard seemed to be in some other language—Japanese, maybe? Were they showing *Just Me and the Kids* reruns in Japan now?

I glanced back at my house. It looked very small and very empty.

You have to leave it tonight, to be able to stay for good, I reminded myself.

Toby said something that I missed, because his voice got lost in the flurry of Japanese inside my head.

"What?" I said.

"I said, I'd feel better driving my own truck," he said. "Your car is probably in better shape, but, I don't know, in all the big city traffic, if I need to react to something in a hurry, I'd be more comfortable in a vehicle I know."

It struck me that that was kind of a long speech for Toby.

"That's fine," I said. "You really think there's going to be bad traffic in the middle of the night?"

"Chicago's a crazy place," Toby said, with a completely straight face. We were beside his pickup now; he held the passenger door open for me.

"Thank you," I said, settling in. It looked like he'd cleaned out the cab of the truck, on my behalf. Everything was very tidy.

Toby slid in behind the steering wheel. I pulled out my Internet directions.

"So here's how you go," I began.

Toby barely glanced at the papers in my hand.

"I'm okay until we get to Chicago," he said. "Then you'll have to navigate."

He turned the motor on and swung out into the dark street. I sat back, only vaguely listening to the Japanese in my head. Soon we were passing nothing but dark farmhouses and empty cornfields. I imagined being a girl from one of those farmhouses, sneaking away to the big city with her boyfriend in the middle of the night. That's probably what we would look like if anyone saw us. I had only a caution-ary-TV-movie version in my head of what would happen to kids like that. They'd get hooked on drugs. The girl would have to sell herself into prostitution. Their parents, left back in the dark farmhouses, would do nothing but weep.

I reminded myself that Toby and I weren't those kids.

Toby cleared his throat.

"I don't know why you trust me," he said.

I looked over at his silhouette in the dark truck. I tried to force back the distracting chatter in my head.

"What?" I said.

"After last night," he said. "After what I did, what Darnell and me did. Kidnapping you. Roz said you probably thought we were going to rape and murder you. She said what we did was as bad as torture, because the whole time you had to be imagining what was going to happen."

I had heard Roz say all that, when I'd been huddled on the couch in the Party Barn and Toby and Darnell were seeking her advice at the end of her shift at Straley's Family Diner. I'd heard it only dimly, because there were worse things going on in my head just then.

"Roz said we terrorized you," Toby continued, as if to torture himself.

"Never mind," I said. "I could tell you meant well. That's why I trust you now."

"You shouldn't take risks like this," Toby said, which was kind of funny, him scolding me for trusting him.

"You shouldn't either," I said in a teasing voice. "Why'd you take the risk of kidnapping me?"

I didn't have much—okay, *any*—experience with how normal conversations were supposed to go between teenagers. But I thought that should be a cue for Toby to laugh and turn everything into a joke, maybe blame me for sitting outside on my balcony and being so easily carried away. That's the way conversations always worked on *Just Me and the Kids*—even the most serious comment had to be followed by a laugh line within a few seconds.

But Toby's face stayed somber. He half-turned to me, only

barely watching the road that stretched out ahead of us.

"I wanted to talk to you about that," he said. "I was hoping I'd get a chance to tell you this tonight."

I gulped.

"Um. Okay," I said.

He didn't say anything. The glow of another car's headlights swept across my face and was gone.

"Well?" I said.

Toby frowned.

"I didn't think my chance would come so soon. I thought I'd have more time to figure out how to say this," he said. He brushed hair out of his face. "Okay, it's this."

I waited.

"It's probably hard for you to understand, because you were on TV from the time you were—what? Six?" he asked.

"Five and a half," I said.

"Five and a half, then. Just about as long as you can remember, you've been somebody. You've already done something important with your life."

He sounded respectful, awed. Impressed.

"I was on a sitcom," I said dryly.

Toby nodded vigorously, missing the sarcasm in my voice.

"Exactly," he said. "You were on national TV. You don't know what it's like to feel like you're nobody and nothing. To know that, odds are, you're never going to amount to anything."

There was an ache in his voice, raw, exposed pain.

"That's how you feel?" I asked doubtfully. This was not how I saw Toby. I'd seen how Roz looked at him, how Darnell treated him. People who were nobody and nothing wouldn't have loyal friends like that.

But Toby was nodding again.

"I'll probably still be delivering furniture and appliances when I'm fifty," he said.

"What about school?" I said. "People go off to college. They get degrees and become engineers. Lawyers. Doctors. Maybe you'll be the person who discovers the cure for cancer!"

I knew I'd said the wrong thing as soon as the words were out of my mouth.

Toby was staring straight out at the road ahead.

"I'm not very good at school," he said. "None of those things are going to happen to me."

"Well, then . . ." I couldn't think of a consolation prize.

Toby looked back toward me.

"Don't you see?" he asked, his voice cracking with earnestness. "That was why I talked Darnell into helping me kidnap you. That was going to be my one good deed, my one achievement, my one big accomplishment. It was something I could do. It was supposed to be the best thing I ever did in my whole life!"

Toby was going to make me cry if I didn't watch out. I couldn't let him stay so serious.

"Why would you waste your one big achievement on me?" I said, trying to sound like I was teasing. "You didn't even know me. Was it just because I used to be a star?"

I overdid the sarcasm. My words came out sounding bitter, almost angry. I tried again.

"Wouldn't I be worth helping out if I was—how'd you put it?—'nobody and nothing'?" I asked.

Toby was quiet for a minute.

"Sure," he said. Then he added softly, "I knew I wouldn't be able to say this right."

I sat there in the dark, listening to the Japanese in my head for a while. I had a sense of hundreds of kids in Tokyo all talking at once. The voices blurred together.

"Toby," I said. "It was just by accident that I got on *Just Me and the Kids.* It wasn't something I planned."

"I know that story," he said. "You just went to the audition because of your babysitter, right?"

I nodded, remembering. After my mother left—an event so far back in time that I didn't even remember it—my father found babysitters for me by posting help wanted signs on the bulletin boards in the English department. I heard him telling another professor once how he chose the right babysitters: "You just ask them what they're majoring in. If it's romantic poetry, you know they're going to be too flighty to remember they're even babysitting a kid. If it's linguistics, they're going to be logical and organized, but not necessarily any fun. The English education majors are always good—unless they're in the midst of student teaching, in which case they're usually too stressed out . . ."

Veronica was a Shakespeare major. She told me—because she told me everything, or at least claimed to, back then— that it wasn't so much that she actually liked Shakespeare. But she wanted to be an actress, a famous actress, and she thought that studying Shakespeare would give her the seriousness she'd been lacking as a California blonde.

She heard about the *Just Me and the Kids* audition from a friend of a friend, and got her hands on a script. We practiced for hours on end, her reading the part of the sexy, single next-door neighbor, me reading everyone else's lines. To me it was just a game, something that was a little bit more interesting than watching her do her homework. I already knew how to read pretty well (thanks to all those education major babysitters I'd had before Veronica) so it wasn't that hard to run through the script again and again. I started doing different voices for all the kids, and a fake-deep macho-sounding voice for the dad.

"Stop! Stop! You're making me laugh!" Veronica always protested.

I liked to make her laugh. I thought the next-door neighbor and the dad in the script would end up getting married, and sometimes I pretended that that was going to happen with Veronica and my dad too. Sometimes I even pretended that it would turn out that Veronica and my dad were already married . . . because she was secretly my mother, but my dad didn't recognize her because it had been so long. And she was trying to work her way back into his good graces, and would one day soon reveal everything. As far as I was concerned, the only thing wrong with that pretense was that I could never figure out why Veronica would have left in the first place.

The day of Veronica's audition I was supposed to have a different babysitter—Natalya, who was not just a linguistics major but strict and Russian, to boot—but she got sick at the last minute and my dad called Veronica.

I was surprised that Veronica said yes, because she'd told me how serious the audition was, how important it was to the entire course of her future. All the way down to the audition, in the heavy Los Angeles traffic, she told me that I had to behave very, very well because she needed to show how good she was with kids. Because when she got the part, she'd be working with kids all the time.

I see now that she was nervous. And maybe I was like a lucky charm for her? A security blanket of sorts? A comfort?

I was not nervous in the least, because I wasn't trying out for anything. I would just be reading the lines with Veronica because she was used to me. I was familiar.

I could tell immediately that there was something wrong at the audition, because everyone was watching me, not Veronica. Veronica stumbled on a line, and I covered for her automatically, without even thinking.

"Well, that's so obvious!" I said. "Everyone knows schist is a type of rock!"

Everyone watching from the side of the room laughed.

"Great ad lib!" one of them muttered, writing on his notepad.

When Veronica's audition was over, a woman came up to her and said they wanted to see me interacting with some of the other kids.

"*Her?*" Veronica practically spat. "She's not trying out."

"Oh, I meant both of you," the woman said smoothly. "Together."

Did Veronica understand right away? Did she understand, but hope, anyway, that they might throw her a bone? A bit part, guest appearances every now and then—*something*?

In the end I was offered a part. Veronica was not.

I was a five-year-old who knew nothing about acting. I didn't have an agent. I didn't have a stage mom or stage dad trotting my pictures around, pushing me out into the spotlight. I was just a five-year-old who would say something like "Well, that's so obvious!" because I'd spent practically my entire life in the presence of adults—adults with doctorates, mostly—rather than other children. In the beginning I wasn't that different from Elizabeth Camplin, my character on the show. I just had fewer siblings and a less-involved dad.

"You were discovered," Toby said now, grinning, as if he wanted to celebrate my good news of eleven years ago with me.

"Yeah, but my babysitter hated me after that," I said, shocking myself. I had never told anyone that. Because Veronica stayed around. She became my stage mom and agent of sorts, serving as go-between between my home and Hollywood.

Did she ever give up hoping that she'd be cast as well?

"She never hurt you, did she?" Toby asked, an unexpected question.

"Not physically," I said.

When I grew into my "talent," I heard a lot of things Veronica said about me. She criticized my hair, my face, my voice, my inflections, my accent, my personality, my intelligence, my physique. (What physique did I even have, at eleven?) I don't think there was a single thing she liked about me, even though she was saccharine sweet to me in person. Whenever we were out together in public, she'd throw her arms around me and proclaim at the top of her voice, "Lindsay's the daughter I never had!"

"Oh," Toby said sympathetically. "The bruises usually heal. The other stuff . . ." He shrugged.

It was strangely cozy, riding with Toby in his truck in the dark. Maybe it was just my imagination, but the Japanese chatter seemed to recede in my mind—background noise rather than a complete distraction. Since I didn't understand any of the words, I could let it blend in with the sound of the tires on the road. I revised my imagined story of the two farm kids running off to the big city. Maybe they wouldn't stop in wicked Chicago, falling into drugs and prostitution. Maybe they'd keep driving, becoming gypsies of sorts. Maybe only good things would happen to them.

When we got into Chicago, finding ourselves on the type of massive multilane freeways I remembered from L.A., Toby tightened his grip on the steering wheel. Semis blew past us—the whole road seemed to be taken up with trucks that dwarfed Toby's pickup. Toby asked for directions through gritted teeth: "Is that exit ramp on the right or the left? . . . What was the number of that highway again? . . . How many miles before the next turn?"

But he got us there. He sat in the truck, waiting, while I rushed into the phone store, the copy shop, and then into a post office lobby to finally place my letter carefully into a mailbox. A sign on the box said that the mail would be picked up next at five a.m.

It was done.

Chapter 16

Toby was quiet driving back toward home on the freeway again. He didn't say anything until we were almost out of the city traffic.

"Want to stop and get something to eat?" he asked.

I calculated. It was still probably another hour and a half home.

"As long as we're back to Springdale by five," I said. I remembered to keep up my pretense. "Mrs. Mullin wakes up about then."

"We'll be fine," Toby said.

He pulled off at an all-night diner that I think was supposed to be called The Stardust, but the lights of the *d*, *u*, and *s* were burnt out on the sign, so it looked like The Star__t. I liked that. The start.

We sat down on puffy booth seats that would have fit in on a soda fountain set in a 1950s period TV show. The table was edged in chrome.

Toby looked around, grinning.

"This is good, eating someplace we don't have at home," he said. "I was afraid we were going to have to settle for McDonald's or Burger King." His grin got bigger. "Do you know, I've never been to Chicago before?"

"Really?" I said, surprised. "Why not?"

He shrugged.

"Why would I have?"

I didn't know. It occurred to me that I knew virtually nothing about Toby. And I hadn't asked.

"But you said Roz had been . . ."

Toby rolled his eyes.

"She won an essay contest when we were in eighth grade," he said. "Got to spend the night in some fancy-schmancy hotel. She wouldn't stop talking about it the rest of the year."

The only time I'd been in Chicago, it'd been during a publicity tour for *Just Me and the Kids.* I'd seen seven malls in two days and said, "That's so obvious!" at least a dozen times. Or had that been Milwaukee?

I remembered that soon after we'd moved to Springdale, Dad had suggested going to Chicago one weekend. It was June, he'd finished grading all the finals, the students had disappeared from Springdale. The air was full of a sense of possibility.

But of course I hadn't gone to Chicago with Dad. *That* hadn't seemed possible. Not when I'd just found my safe house, just escaped the constant noise in my head, just started my new life.

Now I wondered, what if I'd been a little braver? It would have been for only a weekend. What if I'd given Dad a chance? That was the only time he'd ever suggested anything like that.

How was I to know he was going to die?

The sleepy-eyed, overweight waitress came over to the table to give me and Toby each a copy of the worn menus.

"My treat," I told Toby. "Order anything."

He didn't argue. He ended up having blueberry pancakes with sausage and eggs. I had just the blueberry pancakes. They were good, the first food in two weeks that hadn't stuck in my throat. I ordered an extra glass of milk to wash them down.

"The surprise you arranged for Mrs. Mullin—it's something she'll really, really like, right?" Toby asked me.

"She should," I said. "It's for her and her husband, actually. They'll both like it."

Toby twisted his fork in the remains of his eggs.

"But you won't tell me what it is?"

I debated, and then shook my head.

"Nope."

Toby put down his fork.

"It must be nice to have money, to be able to give people things," he said. "Christmas shopping, you can probably go into any store you want, start pulling stuff off the shelf without even looking at the prices. 'I want one of these and one of these and one of these . . .'"

My father and I had never exchanged much in the way of

Christmas presents. Sometimes I'd ordered him a book I'd known he wanted off the Internet. Sometimes, if I told him the right sizes, he'd ordered me new khaki pants or jeans, new nondescript shirts. The gulf between Toby's vision of my life and the reality of it was so huge that I didn't know what to say.

The waitress came back and slid the bill onto our table.

"I know you aren't asking for my advice, but I'll give it anyway," she said. "Because I was you twenty years ago. Go home. Whatever you're running away from isn't worth it."

I gazed up at her, baffled.

Toby picked up the bill.

"We're not runaways," he said with great dignity. "We're going home right now, in fact."

I realized that she'd seen us as those two farm kids running away to adventure. I hadn't known there was yet another alternate ending: The girl ends up alone, as a waitress in an all-night diner, still full of regrets twenty years later.

Toby was already up at the cash register, paying the bill. I made a mental note to slip him a twenty when we got outside.

When we were back on the road, I could hear the waitress telling the cook about us.

Did you see them? The boy was so country, he was wearing cowboy boots. And the girl—bet you anything this was the first time she'd ever worn makeup.

Embarrassed, I rubbed at my cheeks, trying to remove some of the blush.

I think the girl might have been pregnant, the waitress continued. *She ordered two glasses of milk.*

I let out a gasp that, at the last minute, I managed to turn into a cough.

Toby looked over at me curiously.

"Are you all right?" he asked.

"Sure," I said. "I'm fine."

"Sometimes you get this look on your face," he said. "Like you're not really here. You're in some other world. Do all actresses do that?"

I hadn't known Toby could be so observant. How had he noticed so much about me when we were in a dark truck?

"I don't know," I said carefully. "I don't know what other actresses do."

Toby tilted his head to the side.

"Maybe everyone does that," he said. "I know when I was going through . . . kind of a rough spell . . . a few years back, I had this place I could go in my mind. Things I could think about that I knew wouldn't hurt me. Are . . . are things that bad for you now?"

"No," I said, and to my surprise it was the truth. We sped on through the night, and the waitress at the Star__t diner didn't say anything else about me. The foreign jabbering tapered off, and for miles at a time I had my mind to myself. The inside of my head was nearly as quiet as it would have been at home.

Maybe this is what my life could be like, I dared to think. *Maybe I won't have to stay home so much in the future.* It'd been

five years since I'd been in the public eye. People were starting to forget me. That was good. Random comments from
random people like the waitress—I could withstand that,
couldn't I?

I felt safe enough to doze off a little in the dark, cozy
truck, with Toby at the wheel. I leaned my head against the
window.

"You can put your head on my shoulder, if you want,"
Toby said softly. Or maybe he didn't—maybe I only dreamed
it. Either way, it made me smile in my sleep, though I didn't
move my head.

I half-woke up a while later, when Toby stopped for gas.
Groggily I squinted at the digital numbers glowing red on
the dashboard clock. It said 4:17. The glaring lights of the
gas station shone down on me through the windshield, but
the good feeling from my dream stayed with me. I turned
to watch Toby through slitted eyelids. In Hollywood they'd
call his face "chiseled." His chiseled face looked so serious,
so intent as he watched the numbers speeding past on the
gas pump.

Oh. I need to hand him my credit card, I remembered. *I said
I'd pay for gas.*

I heard the voice in my head just as I was leaning down,
reaching into my purse.

Yes . . . yes, it said, so groggily that I knew it had to belong
to someone newly awakened, just like me. I didn't recognize
the voice, but it went on dreamily. *Yes, I have a daughter. I
used to have a daughter. My Lindsay . . .*

Chapter 17

I dropped my purse and put my hands over my ears.

"No," I whimpered. "No."

In the past five years, since I'd come into my "talent," I'd never heard my mother's voice. Not once. Even in the months I'd spent in California, hearing everything, I'd never heard her.

What kind of mother never talks about her daughter?

The same kind who leaves her husband and daughter and never comes back. You know that. So what?

Still, I couldn't make myself unhunch my shoulders, bring my hands down from my ears. Or stop *listening*—my traitorous brain, despite the blocked ears, was still searching out into the distance, reaching for another utterance, however small, from that distinctive voice.

"Stop it," I muttered to myself. "Stop it."

Somehow tears had started rolling down my face, and I finally took my hands off my ears to angrily wipe them away.

Toby opened the door on the other side of the truck.

No! Don't come back yet! Not until I have a chance to pull myself together!

I turned my face to the window, pretending to be sound asleep.

"Lindsay?" Toby whispered.

I didn't move.

He touched my shoulder, shaking it gently.

"I think you're having a nightmare," he murmured. "You're crying in your sleep."

I still didn't move. I could feel Toby hovering over me, could feel his anxiety and worry. He wanted me to wake up and tell him I was only crying over dream troubles, figments of my imagination. I hadn't known you could feel that coming from another person, without even seeing his face. But after a few moments he sighed and sat back behind the steering wheel.

The renewed motion of the truck was good, because it was speeding me toward home, toward silence. I'd been a fool to come so far away; I should have just given the letter to Toby, let him mail it, forgotten about extras like the phone. The rest of the way home I would be totally vulnerable: Anything my mother wanted to say about me, I'd have to hear. I was defenseless.

Why would she start talking about me now? Where is she, anyway? Why . . .

I wouldn't let my mind ask any more questions. I had no memories of my mother. She'd left before anything about her—the sound of her voice, the sight of her face, the feel of her touch—had had a chance to leave an imprint on me. I'd always thought it was better that way. You can't miss what you don't remember. And I hadn't missed her when I'd had all those English-major babysitters doting on me, Veronica playing stage mom, all the makeup artists and hair stylists and fashion consultants and acting coaches taking care of me.

But I didn't have any of that now. And I'd heard my real mother's voice.

It changed everything.

Little kids on the eastern coast of Canada woke up and started watching *Just Me and the Kids* reruns before school.

That girl's stupid!

You're stupid for watching this show!

A grandmother in Florida, up before sunrise for her morning walk, started telling a long, convoluted story to her walking companion.

Remember that little girl who was on that TV show a while back? Lindsay something—Lindsay Scott? Well, our little Isabel looks just like her, except cuter of course, and Dave and Jenny have been talking about getting her into acting. If that Lindsay could do it, so could our Isabel. . . .

A man in prison in Iowa moaned in his sleep, and I heard it. I didn't want to think about why that moan had anything to do with me.

But I didn't hear my mother's voice again. My head rattled

against the hard window, a constant and painful reminder that I couldn't stiffen my neck and straighten up into a sitting position, because then Toby would know that I wasn't asleep. He'd expect me to talk normally and act like a normal person, not like someone who'd just heard a ghost's voice in her head. Every now and then I'd peek out through the cracks between my eyelids, looking for road signs or some other indication of where we were, how far we had left to go. But all I ever saw was darkness, farms draped in darkness, small towns wreathed with it. How could there be so much darkness in the world?

"Lindsay?" Toby whispered. "You're home."

It took me a moment to make sense of his words, to pull them apart from the chatter in my head. I couldn't quite believe it. I'd peeked out just a moment ago, and hadn't seen anything familiar. Springdale had looked just as strange and dark as everywhere else.

I sat up.

"Oh. Er—thanks," I said. "Thanks for taking me."

I could see my house now. I hadn't turned the front light on, so it looked every bit as dark as everywhere else. But that darkness was just a disguise. This was my home, my sanctuary, my guarantee that I wouldn't have to be surprised by my mother's voice again.

"Bye," I said, already halfway out the door, clutching my purse.

"Uh—," Toby said, but I wasn't listening to him. I waved without turning.

"Got to get in before Mrs. Mullin wakes up," I muttered, not really caring if he heard me or not.

I ran up the sidewalk and leaped for the doorstep, aiming headfirst for the blessed silence.

Chapter 18

I hid out.

All that day and into the next—through two cycles of darkness to light, darkness to light—I lurked inside my house like a fugitive. I stayed away from windows and doors, anything that could tempt me outside. I focused on tasks that would keep me from thinking about the trip to Chicago, the time in the truck with Toby, the jolt of hearing my mother's voice. I wrote a six-page paper about images of betrayal in *Julius Caesar*. I wrote a five-page paper exploring the self-deception that must have been necessary for Neville Chamberlain to agree to appeasement with Germany in 1938. I did the entire next week's worth of algebra homework.

Midafternoon on the second day I realized that the rivulets of sweat streaming down my skin weren't just from panic, or from the fear that somehow, even now, even in my own house, my mother's voice could reach me. I was sweating because I was hot. The sun (which I wouldn't look at, because it was outside) was beating down on the thin uninsulated roof of my house, turning my second-story room into an oven.

There's a solution to that, I told myself. *Open the window.*

Did I dare?

I felt incredibly brave leaving my computer and walking to the window. I pulled open the blind, and blinked in the dazzling sunlight. I turned the window latch and raised the window. Fresh air rushed in at me.

There wasn't a screen in this window opening—this was the window I used to climb out onto my balcony, with all its associations and memories.

Why didn't you open your other window, idiot? I asked myself.

I told myself the other window was too close to my desk; air pouring in from that window could too easily spin my papers into disarray, toss my brilliant thoughts about Caesar and Chamberlain to the floor. I was just being logical.

But standing next to this open window felt dangerous. There was nothing tangible there to stop me from just plunging my head through the opening, straining on tiptoes or scrambling out—a foot, then a foot and a half—until I could hear everything the world had to say.

Including, maybe, my own mother talking about me.

I backed away from the window like an animal trainer avoiding a dangerous beast. I sat back down at my desk, but the algebra before me had turned into meaningless symbols. I stared at it until my eyesight blurred. I don't know how long I sat like that before I heard the noise downstairs, an angry banging.

Pound-pound-pound-pound-pound! A second's break. *Pound-pound-pound-pound-pound!*

I didn't walk downstairs to answer the door. I didn't even tiptoe over to the head of the stairs to peek down and try to catch a glimpse of whoever was knocking, or to look out the front window to see if I recognized any cars parked on the street. I just sat still, staring at the unsolvable mysteries of *x* and *y*.

Eventually the knocking stopped. I let my whole body relax, sliding down in my chair.

Then I heard footsteps.

"You!"

My mind and body were slow to catch up. I was still turning around in my chair, still reasoning *Maybe I should shut the window.*

Roz was already climbing in the window.

"How could you?" she asked contemptuously.

"What?" I asked blankly, frozen in place, half-turned in my chair. I mentally ran through a list of my potential offenses: leaving the window open? Not answering the door? I even thought, *Does she know I didn't bother spell-checking my Caesar paper?*

"You really don't know, do you?" Roz asked. She shook her head in disgust, her short hair flying out around her face.

"People like you, you're probably so used to taking advantage of other people, you—"

"I didn't take advantage of anyone," I said quickly.

"Yeah? Didn't you make Toby drive you to Chicago and back, night before last?"

I blinked. Crazily, my mind picked that moment to notice that Roz was actually smaller than me, shorter, more compact. It was only her feistiness that made her seem so formidable. Her feistiness, her blazing eyes, her fierce stance.

"I didn't *make* Toby drive me to Chicago," I said. "I hired him. But he said he only wanted gas money."

Roz snorted.

"Like you'd actually pay," she scoffed.

"But I did! I—" Then I remembered that I'd never actually fished the credit card out of my purse at the gas station, that I'd been too distracted by the waitress's comments after we left the diner to slip him the twenty for the food. "Oh! I just forgot." My purse was balanced at the edge of my desk. I reached in and peeled three twenties from the wad of cash and held them out to Roz. "Here."

Roz stepped across the room and took the money. Her hands were shaking.

"I wish so bad I could just throw this back in your face," she muttered.

"Why don't you?" I challenged, my voice coming out sounding oddly polite. It was like I was reading from a script I didn't understand, and so I couldn't find the right inflections.

"He needs the money," Roz said. "Do you think every-one's rich like you?"

"Well, then—" I reached back into my purse, came up clutching another handful of twenties. "He can have—"

Roz shoved my hands away.

"He doesn't need charity."

For a moment we stared each other down. I lost. I looked away first.

"So that's taken care of," I said stiffly. "It was just an over-sight. A mistake."

Roz collapsed onto the edge of my bed.

"This isn't about the money," she said. She laid the twen-ties down carefully on my flowered bedspread, and glared at me. "He's convinced himself he's in love with you."

She said "love" like it was the name of a disease.

"L-love?" I repeated numbly. I didn't know how to feel about that. Something—my heart?—jumped inside of me, but at the same time I was thinking, *Oh, Toby, no. I'm too much of a mess for you.*

"Yeah. He thinks you need him to take care of you, like you're some delicate little flower that's too fragile for this cruel world," Roz said mockingly. She narrowed her eyes, her glare like a laser beam now. "And I know how people like you are. I've read the tabloids too. Actresses—it's five minutes in love with one guy, five minutes with the next. They take *marriage* vows and break up the next day. So help me, if you break his heart, I'll, I'll . . ."

She didn't seem capable of thinking of a severe enough threat.

I slumped in my chair. There were so many defenses I could throw back at her: *I didn't ask him to fall in love with me. It's not my fault. Why do you assume all actresses are alike? Why do you always think the worst of me? Why is it your business, anyway? Can't Toby take care of himself?* I was getting madder with each imagined question. I settled for the cruelest dig I could think of.

"Are you jealous?" I taunted. "Mad that he's in love with me and not you?"

Roz didn't react the way I expected. She snorted, a sound that I might have taken as amusement, except that her jaw was still tight with anger, her eyes still squinted in indignation.

"Are you kidding?" she asked. "Didn't anyone tell you? Toby's my cousin!"

I stared back at Roz.

"I didn't know that," I said weakly.

"Of course not," Roz said, back to her full-scale fury. "You don't know anything about him. Or me. You think you can just use him and cast him aside and it doesn't matter."

I opened my mouth to object to that—I hadn't used Toby, or cast him aside—but there was no interrupting Roz. She was on a tear.

"You don't know that when Toby was in seventh grade his stepfather beat him so badly that he was in a coma for ten days. He was trying to protect his mother. My aunt. He was trying to keep his stepfather from beating her. It didn't work. He just beat her worse. And—Toby hasn't been quite right ever since."

I gaped at Roz. Why hadn't I seen that about Toby—that wrongness? Roz acted like it was apparent.

But I'm not quite right either. I've got no idea what's normal and what isn't.

"That scar over his eye . . . ," I whispered.

Roz nodded grimly.

"That's the only visible remnant of his beating," she said. "I'm sure you look at him and think, 'Wow, hot guy! I'm there!' But he's a *person*. A person who's been through a lot of pain. He's still damaged."

I remembered what Toby had said to me in the dark, in the truck. "The bruises usually heal. The other stuff . . ."

"I'm sorry," I told Roz. "I'm really sorry."

She frowned.

"You can say that, but . . . Toby had a big test at school yesterday. One that was really, really important, that could determine if he ever gets his high school diploma—and he took it on two hours' sleep because of you."

"I didn't know that!" I wailed. "How would I have known that?"

"You could have *asked*," Roz said acidly. "You could have said, 'Toby, this doesn't create any problems for you, does it, if we go to Chicago in the middle of the night?' You could have said, 'What's convenient for you?'"

It had never occurred to me to ask something like that.

"I'm sorry," I moaned again. I dropped my face into my hands, trying to hide the fact that I was starting to cry again.

"Oh, for—" Roz stood up. Out of the corner of my eye

I saw her walk over to the door into the hall, hesitate for a moment, and then turn right. A minute later she returned with a damp washcloth.

"Here," she said, holding it out to me. "Wipe all that old makeup off your face. You'll feel better."

I lifted the washcloth to my face and rubbed up and down. The cloth came away streaked tan and brown and black and red. Foundation. Eye shadow. Mascara. Lipstick. I remembered that I'd never bothered removing the makeup I'd put on to go to Chicago, to look older.

"*Somebody* needs to take care of you," Roz muttered, taking the washcloth from my hand and scrubbing at the places I'd missed.

I thought about protesting once again that Mrs. Mullin was taking care of me—really! I could revive the lie I'd told Toby; I could say that Mrs. Mullin was at that very moment asleep in a nearby room. But Roz was sharper than Toby. She could see through lies. I was sure that she could feel the complete and utter emptiness of my house, the way every sound echoed so desolately, the way dust settled over everything.

She knew I was alone.

Roz sighed.

"Why do so many people need taking care of?" she asked, attacking what must have been a particularly stubborn patch of smeared makeup along my chin.

I gazed up at her.

"What makes you so strong?" I asked plaintively. "What holds you up?"

Roz considered this, pausing with the washcloth poised over my face.

"Scar tissue," she said.

Chapter 19

Roz made me walk downstairs to get something to eat.

"Do you like scrambled eggs?" she asked, pulling a carton out of the refrigerator. "Er—forget that."

The carton was empty.

Finally she opened a can of chicken noodle soup, poured it in a bowl, and heated it up in the microwave. She slid it in front of me on the table, and popped open a can of the Sam's Choice cola. She poured that into a glass and added the last ice cube left in the freezer.

I obediently took a sip of the soda, slurped soup from the spoon. It all seemed to take a great deal of effort.

"You're awfully skinny," Roz said critically. "When was the last time you had an actual meal?"

"Um . . ." I considered this. "I think yesterday morning in Chicago. With Toby."

Roz frowned.

"But I had a lot to eat then!" I defended myself. "Three big pancakes, two glasses of milk."

Roz rolled her eyes.

"Are you anorexic like all the other stars?"

"No!" I said. "Just . . . sad." The word came out like a whimper. I gestured at the food before me. "This really doesn't even taste good."

"Well, that's what you get for buying Sam's Choice cola and off-brand soup," Roz said.

I made a sound that might have turned into a giggle, if I'd given it a chance. Somehow Roz's sarcasm made it possible to lift another spoonful of the soup to my mouth, to gulp down a large swallow of the soda.

Roz was still watching me.

"It doesn't look like Mrs. Mullin's been staying here at all," she said skeptically. "Was everything you told Toby a lie?"

"No!" I protested.

Roz looked like she was about to challenge me, and I began debating. Was it worth trying to muster up my best acting skills and make my lies more convincing? Or did I maybe . . . possibly . . . want to tell her more of the truth?

But in that next instant there was a loud bang at the front of my house—a bang that turned into a steady pounding.

Someone was knocking at the door just as furiously as Roz had.

"Keep eating," Roz said. "I'll go see who it is."

"You don't have to answer it," I started to say, but by then

Roz had already taken the five steps from the kitchen lino-leum across the living room carpet. She was already swing-ing the door open, saying politely, "Hello, Mrs. Mullin."

I turned around.

The sweet grandmotherly woman I'd seen before had been transformed. She was still wearing a polyester dress—brown this time—and her thick glasses still magnified her startlingly blue eyes. But the emotions magnified in those eyes now weren't sympathy and kindness. They were fury, rage, disdain.

"Uh, it's nice to see you again, Mrs. Mullin," Roz said haltingly.

"You as well, Miss—Tanner, was it?" Mrs. Mullin said ab-sently. Her eyes were focused on me peeking out from the kitchen. "I'm sorry to interrupt, but I really must speak with Lindsay alone." Both Roz and I froze, and Mrs. Mullin added, "Right now."

"Oh, er—" Roz kept looking at me, like she was trying to ask with her eyes, *Is that all right? Or do you need me to stay and provide moral support? Or . . . should I call the police?*

I kept my face carefully blank.

"All right," Roz said. "See you later, Lindsay."

Roz walked out the front door, pulling it gently shut behind her. As soon as she was gone, Mrs. Mullin walked toward me and dropped something on the table in front of me.

It was a letter. A letter with a Chicago postmark, addressed to Dr. Elgin Mullin.

Chapter 20

"He's in a wheelchair," Mrs. Mullin said. "Barely able to move. If he'd seen that letter before I did, if he'd opened it, seen what you were offering him . . . How could you be so cruel?"

I had a choice: play dumb or confess. I went with the easiest reaction, the one that came most naturally.

"What are you talking about?" I asked. "What's that letter got to do with me? What is it, anyway?"

Mrs. Mullin's magnified eyes only grew angrier. Not even the slightest hint of doubt crossed her expression. What did she do—have the letter fingerprinted? Had I accidentally left some other telltale clue?

I thought through every word I'd written in the letter, even considered the generic paper I'd printed it on. I'd been at a copy shop in Chicago—nothing should have pointed back to me.

I decided to try for a little distraction.

"*Who's* in a wheelchair?" I asked. "Dr. Elgin Mullin? Is that—is that your husband?"

On the whole I thought my acting was strong. I'd done a very good job of funneling my bafflement over Mrs. Mullin into the question about her husband. I picked up the letter, pretending to examine the address.

Mrs. Mullin snatched the letter out of my hands. She ripped it in half, dropped the pieces to the floor.

"To think that I felt sorry for you!" she said. "I was trying to help you—I was even trying to go slowly, so you wouldn't be under too much of a strain. And this is the thanks you give me! Involving my husband! Promising things you can't deliver!"

"There's something in that letter that . . . promises something . . . your husband can't have?" I asked, only partly having to fake my befuddlement. "Because he's in a wheelchair?"

I wanted to say that surely there were handicapped-accessible archaeological dig sites somewhere in Greece or Turkey, but I didn't want to give anything away. And, well, maybe there weren't. Maybe my letter was cruel.

Was it my fault the Google search hadn't turned up any information about his disability?

"All his life Elgin wanted to go to Turkey," Mrs. Mullin said, softening a little. "He taught archaeology for thirty years. . . . We'd saved up. We had plane tickets for a flight the week after he retired. And then, the day before his retirement party . . ."

"What happened?" I asked.

"Car wreck," Mrs. Mullin said, and now she sounded almost matter-of-fact, as if she'd had to tell this story so many times that the emotion had gone out of it. "Some kid was a little too eager to go celebrate the end of finals. He ran a red light—it's called a T-bone collision, when you hit someone exactly in the side like that."

"I didn't know," I said. "I'm sorry." Was I going to have to spend the whole day apologizing for things I didn't know? I remembered that I had an act to keep up. I used my foot to nudge the torn edge of the letter Mrs. Mullin had thrown on the floor. "But what does this have to do with me?"

Mrs. Mullin just looked at me.

"You know the answer to that," she said slowly. "But there's a lot you don't know. Because you're trying so hard not to listen. . . ."

I froze. Just what did Mrs. Mullin know? And how did she know it? The room seemed to spin around me a little bit. I clutched the edge of the table, trying to steady myself.

"Friday morning," Mrs. Mullin said, "our dog started scratching at the door to be let out. Weak bladder. Happens a lot when you get old, whether you're a dog or a human. I could sympathize." She watched my face, waiting for some sort of reaction. I couldn't understand why we were suddenly talking about incontinent dogs.

"The dog has a little bit of trouble walking, too," Mrs. Mullin continued. "So I carried her out to the backyard. It must have been three, three thirty in the morning. We live out on the very edge of Springdale, practically in the country. Usually it would be really quiet in our backyard, in the middle of the night, but I could hear voices, two kids talking, a boy and a girl."

I gasped. I could practically feel the blood draining from my brain, the color draining from my face. I felt devastated. Faint. And maybe a little bit relieved?

"You heard us?" I whispered.

Chapter 21

I couldn't stop gaping at Mrs. Mullin. Her eyes widened, a show of innocence.

"Were you in my backyard?" she asked.

"No. We—"

"You and that boy must have been a hundred miles away," Mrs. Mullin said, shaking her head. "In Chicago, right? Mailing my husband's letter? How could I have heard you two talking?"

She smiled.

"Please!" I said. "This is important!"

"So is my husband," Mrs. Mullin said. "So was your father. So is your mother."

I started gasping for air. Did Mrs. Mullin say "So are you," or did I just imagine it over the ringing in my ears?

"Lindsay?" Mrs. Mullin said. She peered around frantically,

and then awkwardly bent down to pick up one of the torn envelope halves from the floor. She lifted it to her mouth, blew some air into it to puff it open, and then placed it against my face. "You're hyperventilating. Try to breathe slower."

I breathed in and out, taking my air from the envelope half cupped over my mouth and nose. The ringing in my ears began to fade. But my thoughts kept racing.

I pushed her hand and the envelope away.

"You have to tell me," I said. "I'm not the only one, am I? And don't say, 'Not the only one what?' Because you *know*, and I know, you've got to be just like me. . . ."

"Not exactly alike," Mrs. Mullin said, with just the hint of a smile. "But yes, you are not the only one who can hear things you shouldn't be able to hear."

She was watching me with sympathy again, her kind grandmotherly look back in full force behind the magnification of her glasses.

"So you hear—you heard—" I couldn't get the words out.

"You want another example?" she asked. "I heard Roz saying you'd said I was taking care of you. Didn't you like how I helped you cement that impression the other day?"

I stared at her, open-mouthed. Did she expect me to say thank you? I couldn't think that coherently yet.

"But how—why—wha—" I didn't know where to start. I flailed my arms out, and my right hand hit against the glass of soda, toppling it. The brown liquid streamed across the table and flowed toward the floor. When I didn't react— even to set the glass upright—Mrs. Mullin began a slow, old-ladyish hobbling toward the kitchen counter.

"No, don't worry about that!" I said. "It doesn't matter. I want you to answer my questions!"

Mrs. Mullin didn't stop. She grabbed a handful of paper towels and began dabbing up the spilled soda.

"You're awfully careless about making messes," she muttered.

"Okay! Okay!" I grabbed some of the paper towels, finished cleaning up. "Now . . ."

Mrs. Mullin narrowed her eyes. Shook her head.

"I think I've told you just about enough for now," she said.

"What?" I said.

This was like reading a book and discovering that the last chapter—the one that explained everything—was torn out. No, it was like arriving for your first day of kindergarten and being told after five minutes, "That's it, you're done. That's all we'll ever teach you." No, this was like . . .

Well, really, it wasn't like anything I could think of. It was incredible.

"It can be overwhelming, getting too much information all at once. You should know that, given what you must hear anytime you leave your house," Mrs. Mullin said calmly. She turned toward the door.

I grabbed her arm.

"No! Wait! You can't leave now!"

Mrs. Mullin did not shake my hand off her arm, did not pull away. But she fixed me with a look that made it clear:

Even if I held her hostage, even if I *tortured* her, Mrs. Mullin would tell me no more than she wanted to.

"Please," I begged. I let go of Mrs. Mullin's arm. I picked up the other half of the torn letter from the floor. I tried a different tack. "I wasn't trying to upset your husband. I just didn't know. I thought this would be a good thing—like a gift. A very expensive gift."

Mrs. Mullin frowned.

"A gift that would help you most of all, because it would effectively get rid of that nosy old lady who won't leave you alone," she muttered.

"I never said that!" I protested, thinking back. I hadn't said anything like that to Toby, of course, but what if I'd muttered it to myself, writing the letter? Or standing at the copy shop, waiting for the letter to come out of the printer?

"I'm not stupid," Mrs. Mullin said. "I'm capable of interpreting information, not just hearing it."

She stepped past me. I sprang up, placed myself between her and the door.

"Listen!" I said. "It won't do you any good to leave because . . ." I was feeling a little frantic now. I went back to the threatening approach. "What's to stop me from following you home?"

"You don't drive. I live on the other side of Springdale. It'd be a long walk," Mrs. Mullin said.

"So?" I said. "I know how to walk."

"You'd have to be outside for quite a while," Mrs. Mullin said.

I swayed a little—I really should have eaten more than just a few spoonfuls of soup. But I tried a repeat performance of my insolent "So?" It came out sounding pale and bleached out. Pitiful.

"You don't like being away from home in the middle of the afternoon," Mrs. Mullin said, more gently.

I sagged against the wall.

"How did you know?" I asked. I thought of the man in prison in Iowa, who never missed the three o'clock *Just Me and the Kids.* I thought about the kind of things he always said. It was odd—what he said wasn't exactly graphic, but his tone was always so fervent, so impassioned. So terrifying.

Now I gasped at Mrs. Mullin. "You don't hear it too, do you? Everything people say about me?"

If Mrs. Mullin had been about half a century younger, I would have said that she rolled her eyes at me. On someone her age it looked more like a fluttering of the eyelids.

"Don't flatter yourself," she said. "I only hear the references to myself." Her face softened. "Remember when we were making arrangements for the funeral? You were so concerned, that it couldn't be at certain times."

It had almost slipped my mind, how Mrs. Mullin had helped me with my father's funeral. She'd told me which funeral home to contact, which coffin to buy, which "embalming package" to agree to. I'd been so relieved then, in my dazed state, not to have to make any decisions on my own. The timing of the funeral was probably the only detail I'd said anything about.

Strangely, the memory of Mrs. Mullin's kindness only made me more defiant now.

"What if I walked into your house at three?" I asked. "Isn't it a safe zone too?"

Mrs. Mullin raised an eyebrow.

"How do you know it'd be a safe zone for you?" she asked. "Maybe it is, maybe it isn't. Are you willing to take that risk?"

Mrs. Mullin reached for the door handle.

"Just tell me a little more," I pleaded. I did my best to distill all the questions swirling in my head down to something Mrs. Mullin might answer, something I really wanted to know. "I heard you talking to someone, asking them to check something about me. And then, not long after that, I heard my mother's voice, for the first time since I was a baby, and she was saying yes, she has a daughter. Her Lindsay." I couldn't help allowing a certain amount of bitterness into my voice. I forced myself back on track. "But I couldn't hear who you were talking to, or who my mother was talking to. And I couldn't tell where my mother was, which is kind of weird, because usually I can. Know where people are when they talk about me, I mean. So—"

"This sounds like it's working up to be a lot more, not just a little," Mrs. Mullin said.

I ignored the interruption.

"Do you know where my mother is?"

"I can't tell you that right now," Mrs. Mullin said. At least she said it apologetically.

"Then can you tell me who you were talking to? Who was talking to my mom? If there's a connection between—?"

"There is," Mrs. Mullin said, turning the door handle firmly and stepping out onto my doorstep. "I was talking to the same person your mother was talking to."

I stayed so close behind her that I was in danger of knocking her over. Until she took one more step, down from my doorstep to the sidewalk.

"Who was it?" I asked plaintively, staying in my doorway.

Mrs. Mullin half-turned around. In her face I could see sympathy battling with resolve. I was rooting for sympathy to win.

"What does that person know about me?" I pressed anxiously. "What does he—or she—know about my mother? Why couldn't I hear the other side of the conversation, either time?"

"Why don't you ask her yourself?" Mrs. Mullin said. She resumed walking. She was already to her car by the time I figured out that she meant I should ask her fellow conversationalist, not my mother.

"Wait!" I said. "How do I find this person? How—"

"That's the easy part," Mrs. Mullin said, pulling her car door open. "She lives right across the street."

And with one shaky, arthritic finger, she pointed.

Chapter 22

Mrs. Mullin got into her car and pulled away. I barely noticed.
I just stood in my doorway with my mouth hanging open,
and stared at the house on the other side of the street. It
was every bit as nondescript as my own, practically a twin—
a small one-and-a-half-story wood-framed house, its only
adornment a flat-roofed section that could be considered
a balcony. The biggest difference was that the house across
the street was painted a soft butter yellow, which counted as
a dramatic splash of color on this street full of white- and
cream-colored houses.

I kept standing in my doorway, staring.

I'd probably looked out at that house at least once a
day for the past five years, but I'd never *really* looked at it.
Were the curtains always drawn in all the windows? Were

those shadows I could see moving behind the curtains—or was it just my imagination?

I didn't know who lived in that house. I didn't know any of my neighbors—I'd done everything I could, in the past five years, not to.

Well, that's something you could find out easily enough, I told myself.

I closed the door and raced upstairs, back to my computer. I typed an address—only one digit off from my own—into a cross-referencing phone book site.

Nothing came up.

"Figures," I muttered.

I went to the county auditor's website instead. I'd had to do a project for an online class once about what records local governments are required to provide to the public—not the most exciting topic, but useful at the moment.

Two minutes later I knew that the house across the street from my own was 1135 square feet, on a lot that measured forty by eighty. It had two bedrooms and one bath.

And it had been owned since 1948 by Althea Gooding.

I immediately plugged the name Althea Gooding into every search engine I could think of.

Nothing.

Nothing.

Nothing.

I slumped in my chair, stymied.

You are probably wondering why I didn't immediately

march across the street, rap loudly on my neighbor's door, and begin demanding information. I'd been an actress, after all—surely I could have improvised my way through any situation.

But I'd also been in hiding for the past five years. I'd been incurious.

I read an article for psychology class once about how differently people react when they're given a diagnosis of terminal illness. A certain percentage of people will throw themselves into research, seeking out ever more obscure data, becoming practically as expert as the experts themselves.

Other people don't ask a single question. They won't go to support groups, don't listen at patient information sessions, won't even read doctor's office brochures. They'd just as soon never know what's killing them.

When it came to my secret talent, I was like that second group. For my academic career I could dredge up a decent amount of curiosity about the workings of the stock market, the tulip mania of the Netherlands in the seventeenth century, the lives of Aeschylus and Homer and Alexander the Great and Constantine and all sorts of other people who'd died hundreds or thousands of years before I was born. At least, I could stay curious about them long enough to take a test or write a paper or assemble a project.

But I'd never so much as Googled "hearing voices," "exceptionally strong hearing," or "ESP."

I think, psychologically speaking, this is known as avoidance.

"I can't go," I said aloud. "I won't."

Everything that had happened today, everything that I'd found out—Toby thinking he was in love with me, Roz yelling at me, Mrs. Mullin knowing my secret, Mrs. Mullin yelling at me—all that had happened because I'd stepped out of my ordinary life. I'd taken risks. I should have known it was too dangerous to write the letter to Dr. Mullin, to go to Chicago with Toby, even to eat at the Star__t diner. It would be even more dangerous to walk across the street and talk to Althea Gooding. I needed to stick with what was simple and safe and known—and totally unrelated to me and my secret abilities. Like my papers about the secrets in *Julius Caesar*, the self-deception of Neville Chamberlain.

Secrets, I thought. *Self-deception.*

"NO!" I roared, sweeping the neatly stacked papers to the floor. Those papers weren't really about Julius Caesar or Neville Chamberlain. They were about *me*.

I heard a noise outside my open window just then. It might have been a squirrel scampering along the eaves or a sparrow rising through the oaks or just the wind scattering old dried-out leaves across the balcony. But it didn't sound quite like any of those. It sounded more distinct, more deliberate, more . . . human.

I raced to my window and shoved my head out into the open air. I wasn't careful—I pushed my head a little too far and heard Toby saying, wistfully, *She's really pretty, don't you think?* I pulled my head back a bit, but kept turning it, side to side. To the left there was nothing unusual: the empty expanse of the far side of my balcony, the yard, the street, the yellow house I planned never to visit. I turned my head in the other direction.

To the right I saw Roz.

She was crouched on the narrow edge of the balcony between my window and the stairs that led down to the ground. She had her back shoved up against the house, her head turned slightly, her ear pressed against the wall. Her eyes were wild, darting about; shock and astonishment twisted her face.

She knew.

Chapter 23

As soon as she saw me, Roz started scrambling to stand up, stumbling a bit in her amazement. I reached out and grabbed her arm, pinning her in place. Roz was a lot easier to hold on to than Mrs. Mullin.

"What did you hear?" I demanded.

"I—I—I forgot I left Toby's money on your bed," she said, avoiding my question. And my gaze. Her eyes kept darting about, looking for escape. "I realized as soon as I drove around the corner."

I looked past her, to where her ramshackle car was parked crookedly on the side street, in front of my father's car. She kept talking. Babbling, really.

"I didn't think you'd mind if I came back and got it—the money, I mean," she said. "I didn't want to interrupt you and Mrs. Mullin, since it looked like you were going to be having a pretty serious conversation. I knew you'd left this window open. I was just going to sneak up the back stairs, grab the money, and go."

"But you didn't," I said, like a prosecuting attorney who knows she's got an unbeatable case.

Roz shook her head, the motion jerky and nervous. Her short hair flew out in all directions.

"I could hear that you were arguing, you and Mrs. Mullin," she said, a bit robotically, like someone in shock. "I was worried about you. I—I thought maybe if I listened, I could do something to help."

I wished my special talents included lie detection. Did I believe her? I thought about the people who sneaked around celebrities' homes in Hollywood, digging through their garbage cans to find things to sell on eBay. Justin Timberlake's half-eaten French toast, Ashley Tisdale's toenail clippings.

"Is it true?" Roz gasped. Now she was staring me straight in the eye, her need to know winning out over her urge to get away. "Do you hear . . . things?"

I dropped my grip on Roz's arm. I pulled my head back in through the window opening.

"Leave me alone!" I shouted at her. "Don't ever bother me again!"

My hands shaking, I clutched the top of the window frame. I jerked my arms down, slamming the window shut. I twisted the clasp, locking it tight.

"Lindsay?" Roz said from the other side of the glass. She pressed her face close to the window.

I yanked the blind down as far as it would go.

I stood still, waiting . . . waiting . . .

I listened hard, straining my ears. After a few seconds I heard footsteps descending the stairs on the other side of my wall.

Good, I thought. *Get out of here.*

The footsteps seemed to be running now, a rapid *tap-tap-tap* against the wood, then against the sidewalk. It was amazing—I'd scared off Roz, who was never flustered, who understood everything. She didn't understand me. She couldn't.

Was that a car door I heard scraping open? I could picture her scrambling into her little car, the one with the side-view mirrors held on with duct tape, the muffler held together with baling wire. I was waiting to hear the engine screech into action, in order to carry her back to her own life, so full of people, and leave me safe and alone in mine.

Full of people . . .

Full of people . . .

I whirled around and dashed out of my room, through the hall, toward my stairs. I took them three at a time, plunging down to my living room. I hit the floor at the bottom too hard; my ankles buckled. I struggled to keep my balance, righted myself, flung myself toward the door. I yanked it open.

"Don't tell anyone!" I yelled out into the bright, hot day. "Don't tell anyone!"

Chapter 24

I was too late. Roz's car was already puttering down the side street, already going too fast for me to chase it, even if I dared.

I collapsed in my doorway, my feet sliding out onto the concrete doorstep, my rear end landing hard against the bare living room floor. I dropped my head into my hands, then lifted it slightly, to peek out at my tiny front yard. How long did I have before the newly greening grass would be trampled by paparazzi, before there were faces pressed against all my windows, voices calling, "Lindsay Scott! Lindsay Scott! We know you're in there! Just come out and make a statement, and then we'll leave you alone!"

Except they wouldn't ever leave me alone. There'd be a permanent media circus camped out on my front yard for the rest of my life. Unless I surrendered my every last shred of privacy, I'd be trapped in here like the Texans who died at the Alamo, like the Zealots at Masada.

Who would tell first, Mrs. Mullin or Roz?

Mrs. Mullin, I realized belatedly, had already known for a while. Who could say when she'd figured me out—at my father's funeral? The first time she'd heard of me? If she was going to tell, it would have happened already; the paparazzi would already have been here. And anyhow, outing me would also mean outing herself. She wasn't going to do that.

For one short, evil moment I considered a diversionary tactic if any cameras showed up. I could pull out my best acting skills, stand before the whole wide world on live TV, and say with wide-eyed, faked innocence, "Oh, no, I'm not the freak with the disabling talent. I'm just a former celebrity who likes her peace and quiet. Roz got things mixed up. The only person who can hear voices she shouldn't be able to hear is Mrs. Mullin. That's *M-U-L-L-I-N*, and you can find her at . . ."

But even if I could stoop that low *(could I stoop that low?)*, it wouldn't work. The tabloids weren't interested in gossip about old-lady English department secretaries. They were interested in people like me: young, pretty (well, formerly), fallen, tainted by scandal (or, at least, failure), swarming with secrets.

I clutched my hair in my hand, pulled the strands forward

so they almost completely covered my face. With my head bent down, my face against my knees, some of the longer locks hung all the way down to my ankles. I probably looked as hairy as Bigfoot. This wasn't the worst of it, but I could just imagine what my former costars and acquaintances in Hollywood would say about my appearance: *Look at those split ends! Look at that blotchy skin! Look at those eyebrows—do you think she's waxed them even once in the past five years? . . . How can she stand looking at those hands without a manicure? . . . Okay, I know she's in Rubesville, USA, but can't she find some clothes that look better than that?*

Rubesville, USA . . . I felt a little defensive on Springdale's behalf. It wasn't the town's fault I never went shopping.

Or was it?

A new thought occurred to me. If Mrs. Mullin and I could both hear the voices of anyone talking about us, and this Althea Gooding across the street at least knew about people like us . . . and Springdale had at least two houses that protected people like me . . . and I kind of suspected that Althea Gooding's house might be like that too . . . then what if it was just a Springdale thing? Dad had said that my mother's family came from here, after all. What if pretty much everybody in town was like me, or at least knew people like me? What if my dear absentminded professor father had just neglected to mention this to me because he hadn't known I was one of them? What if, around here, my talent was no big deal?

I remembered the shock and horror in Roz's face, right

before she tried to run away from me. Not everyone around here knew about people like me.

But did Roz live in Springdale?

I realized I didn't know where she lived. It could be Springdale or one of the towns nearby or out in the country—somewhere beyond the boundaries of any Springdale secrets. *Not that I know what those boundaries are,* I thought grimly. *Or what all Springdale's secrets are. Or* . . . I frowned and made myself focus on Roz. Somehow I pictured her living in a trailer park. I based this on the apparent cheapness of her jeans, her job as a waitress, her falling-apart car, the way she'd clutched the three twenty-dollar bills for Toby and snarled, "Do you think everyone's rich like you?"

I moaned, lowering my head even farther between my knees, sweeping my hair against the ground.

Roz needs money. And . . . some tabloids pay.

I imagined Roz auctioning off my secret. She'd handle the bidding well, playing off one publication against another. Who wanted the story the most? The *National Enquirer*? *Look*? *In Style*? *People*? *Us*? Maybe she'd go high-end, classier—was *Vanity Fair* one of the places that paid?

Roz wouldn't do that, I told myself. *She's nice. She takes care of people.*

But she didn't care about me as much as she cared about certain other people. To her I was just a rich, troublesome, needy, psycho actress. If she sold me out, she could get college money for herself and her stepsister and Darnell and Toby and probably five or six other kids. She could pay for therapy for Toby to deal with the aftermath of his stepfather's beating. She could buy her mom a new trailer. Maybe even a house.

I moaned again. Leaning my head so far down, for so long, was making me dizzy. I was starting to see stars. I sat up again and weakly tilted my head against the door frame. Even if Roz didn't sell me out to the tabloids directly, it was inevitable: she would tell *someone*. It'd be too hard for her not to. And even if she said, "Can you keep this secret?" that person would have to tell somebody else. And so on, and so on, a constantly spreading web, until the news reached the first blog or tabloid and it all snapped back on me, trapping me in my house. I'd be imprisoned by paparazzi for the rest of my life. The process was probably already beginning—Roz could be on her cell phone right now, even as she drove, telling the first person. There was nothing I could do to stop her.

But could I do anything to prepare?

Across the street the butter yellow house belonging to Althea Gooding seemed to gleam in the sunlight, like a beacon. Fifteen minutes ago I'd resolved never to step foot in that house, never to even knock at its door. But everything had changed in the past fifteen minutes. Hiding in my own house wasn't safe or easy anymore.

Could I hide at Althea Gooding's?

Chapter 25

Walking down my sidewalk, across the street, and then up toward Althea Gooding's doorstep felt like a journey of epic proportions. Moses leading the Israelites out of Egypt, Philippides running the first marathon, John Glenn blasting off to orbit the earth—none of those people could have felt as anguished, as traumatized, as *terrified* as I did, just taking those twenty or so steps.

Part of it was that I couldn't help listening. With each step forward I expected to hear Roz or someone else saying, *Hello? National Enquirer?* Or—and somehow this seemed nearly as bad—Toby saying, *Are you kidding? She can do that? What a weirdo! That's sick!* I walked briskly, though, and heard only the usual chatter. *The one where she laughs so hard that milk squirts out her nose—that's my favorite episode. . . .*

No, she only says milk squirts out her nose. Remember? And then there's this huge fight? . . .

What do you think that kid was making at the height of that show? More or less than the Olsen twins? . . .

One concrete sidewalk square away from Althea Gooding's doorstep, I paused and glanced back at my house. This felt momentous—like it might be my last chance to see my home before it was overrun by the media hordes.

My house didn't look like it was about to be invaded. It looked peaceful, calm, inviting. I almost turned around and went back.

Lot's wife turned into a pillar of salt when she looked back, I reminded myself. *Learn from her mistakes.*

Boldly I took two quick steps forward, landing on the doorstep. Instantly the voices in my mind fell silent. I grinned.

It's true! I exulted. *This is another safe house!*

I wondered if Christopher Columbus had felt this jubilant, watching land approach from the deck of the *Santa Maria.*

I remembered that Christopher Columbus had been completely wrong about exactly what he'd discovered. My grin faded.

I raised my hand to knock at the white wooden door. I flexed my wrist. My knuckles brushed the door as gently as a spring breeze, as lightly as a feather's touch. This was ridiculous: I'd have to do better than that. Althea Gooding couldn't have heard that knock even if she'd been standing right on the other side of the door with her ear pressed against the wood.

I knocked again, putting more force behind it. *The charac-ter you're playing is confident. Assured. In control,* I told myself. My knocks echoed down the empty street. And then there was an answering echo from inside: footsteps.

I once acted in a scary movie—it was on the Disney Chan-nel, nothing too extreme—but the director had a hard time getting me to scream fearfully enough. He made me practice again and again; I screamed until my vocal cords were raw. But I never really quite got it. I didn't understand what it was like to be afraid, back then.

I could scream right now, quite easily.

The footsteps came slowly toward me. I fell into an agony of waiting between each step, because each one seemed to be the last, and each time I was sure the door was about to be whipped open. But then there'd be another step. And another.

"Yes?" the muffled voice came from behind the door. "Who's there?"

It sounded like a woman, a very old woman. *Well, duh,* I thought nervously. *She bought the house in 1948. That was a long time ago.* The voice reminded me a bit too much of the witch in *Hansel and Gretel.*

"I-It's Lindsay, uh, Lindsay Curran," I stammered, com-pletely falling out of character. "M-Mrs. Mullin said I should talk to you?"

"Yes." She hissed the *s* at the end. The door slowly creaked open. "Come in."

I blinked. Everything in the house was so dim after the

bright sunlight that it took my eyes a few moments to focus. And I had to look down, because the woman standing before me was tiny, child-size.

I had thought that Mrs. Mullin was very old—and she was, by Hollywood standards. But this woman made Mrs. Mullin look almost youthful. This woman was so ancient that her skin looked practically translucent, held together only by the wrinkles. Her halo of white hair seemed to glow with its own unearthly light. And her dark deep-set eyes looked like they might have seen the beginning of time.

"Althea Gooding," the woman said, slowly raising one fragile-looking hand. It took me a moment to realize I was supposed to shake it.

"L-Lindsay Curran," I said, forgetting that I'd already introduced myself. I clasped her hand gingerly. It was like trying to hold on to fine china or rare glass. I could feel the bones under her wrinkles, and feared I might break them just with a touch.

"Come, child," Althea said. "Come."

She pulled me in, over the threshold. Really, "pulled" is much too strong a word—it was like being tugged on by a gnat's wing, by a whisper. But I stepped onto the warped floor, feeling the waviness of the wood through the soles of my shoes.

Althea peered out the door behind me, the way soldiers under siege might peek out into terrifying darkness. And yet the sun was as bright and glorious as ever, the sky full of bird-song. She swung the door shut with a firmness I wouldn't have thought she was capable of.

My eyes were adjusting to the dimness of the house, behind all those heavy drapes. Like me, Althea Gooding used her front room as a living room—no, in her case, I think the proper term would be "parlor." A stiff Victorian-era couch and matching chair, both upholstered in deep burgundy velvet, stood before the fireplace. A glassed-in wooden case held books with Roman numerals on their spines. A vast table that Lincoln and his cabinet could have used to plot Civil War strategy stood behind the couch. I played a little game with myself: I tried to find one item in the room that could have been manufactured after 1948, after the year that Althea Gooding bought the house. I failed. I decided that Mrs. Mullin, in her dated polyester dresses, must look jarringly modern every time she went to visit Althea Gooding.

"Tea?" Althea offered.

"Um, sure," I said.

She poured it from a china teapot decorated with delicate roses. She sat on the chair, and I perched on the couch. *This is what it would have been like visiting Emily Dickinson*, I thought. *If she'd lived to be an old, old lady.*

I was trying to think what to start with, which of the dozens of questions tangled in my mind I should begin trying to unravel, when Althea suddenly chirped, "Thaddeus Clay."

"Excuse me?" I said, dribbling out my lukewarm tea.

"He was the first one," she said.

"The first one what?" I asked.

Althea regarded me disapprovingly, her head tilted, her lips pursed.

"You mean . . . the first one like . . . me and Mrs. Mullin?" I ventured. The disapproval in Althea's eyes barely softened. "And . . . you?" I tried again.

"Of course," Althea said. I wasn't sure which part she was saying "of course" to.

"Oh," I said. "I didn't know. . . ."

"You know who settled Springdale, don't you?" she asked suddenly, as if I hadn't even spoken. I was beginning to feel like I was talking with a character Alice might have met in Wonderland or through the looking glass—the Red Queen, maybe?

"I do," I said, reminding myself that I was supposed to be visualizing my character here as someone very confident and self-assured. Assertive. "Springdale was settled by idealists from the East Coast, wanting to create their own utopia."

"And?" Althea prompted, like a teacher ready to scold a student who clearly hadn't studied.

"And what?" I said. "Idealists. Utopians. You don't want a list of actual names, do you?"

"No." Althea shook her head, grim now. "But what did they believe? What were their ideals? What was going to make up their utopia?"

"I'm sorry," I said. "I don't—"

"They were transcendentalists," Althea cut me off, hissing her s sounds again.

"Oh, right," I said. I guess I'd known that. But I had sort of a mental block about transcendentalists because of Dad. It was like having a father you hated who was a football coach, so you hated football, too.

Not that I'd *hated* Dad, exactly. It was more that we'd just existed on separate planes. He didn't get me; I didn't get him. And transcendentalism . . . Well, as far as I'm concerned, even the experts were probably just faking when they said they understood. It's too nebulous. Look up "transcendentalism," and there's a lot of mushy blather about literature, culture, religion, politics, philosophy, and "new ideas," circa 1836. Right. Whatever. Academics have written entire books about who should and shouldn't properly be counted as transcendentalists. Emerson and Thoreau, in; Nathaniel Hawthorne, out. I know because my father had owned all those books. He'd pored over them late into the night practically every single night, scrawling notes to himself in the margins of every page, licking his fingers to turn the pages.

Was I just jealous? Jealous that he'd given so much attention to transcendentalism and ignored me?

I forced myself to focus back on Althea's ancient, deep eyes. *Transcendentalists in Springdale*, I reminded myself. *Don't think about Dad.*

"I thought the transcendentalist movement was centered in Massachusetts," I said, like a desperate student clutching at straws, hoping for partial credit.

Althea frowned at me. "The public face of transcendentalism was in Massachusetts," she said scornfully. "The publicity hounds."

"So the ones who wanted privacy came to Springdale?" I countered. "The crazy ones who heard voices in their heads and didn't want anyone to know?"

Althea blinked at me, a movement as subtle as a moth opening and closing its wings.

"They were trying to hear the voice of God," she said.

The suddenly reverent look on her face stopped me from shooting off a sarcastic comeback.

"Do you know Emerson's views on language?" she asked. "The connections he saw between God and man and words and nature? 'This relationship between the mind and matter is not fancied by some poets, but stands in the will of God, and so is free to be known by all men.'"

This is a fairly famous quote, transcendentally speaking, but I never really thought it meant anything. Althea still looked reverent, but I couldn't hold back the sarcasm anymore.

"Oh, of course," I said. "That's why I always hear gossip in my head."

Althea looked down at the teacup and saucer balanced in her hands.

"God is too big for most of us," she whispered. "Humans are very self-centered."

It wasn't the Red Queen or Emily Dickinson I'd gone to visit. It was the Sphinx. The Sphinx with all those maddening riddles.

"What's that supposed to mean?" I demanded.

"When we listen for God, what do we want to hear?" she asked, the force of her breath making concentric circles in her tea. "Are we concerned about the state of the universe? The state of humanity? No. Not truly. Each one of us really wonders, 'What does God think of me?'" She straightened up, stared back at me. "The early Springdale settlers said they were listening for God. But all they ever wanted to hear was each other."

For a moment I could almost picture it, a bunch of nineteenth-century figures in plain wooden pews, the men in dark hats, the women and girls in calico dresses with sunbonnets knotted around their necks. They all had their heads bowed, and looked to be devoutly in prayer. But secretly they were all peeking and eavesdropping, each one listening for his or her own name.

"But *how*?" I said. "People aren't supposed to be able to hear so much! Being able to hear other people, far away . . . It's not a useful adaptation." For a moment I wondered if Althea Gooding had ever heard of Darwin and evolution, or if that was too modern for her. I decided I didn't care. "How could this Thaddeus Clay just develop his abilities, just like that, out of the blue?"

Althea regarded me levelly.

"How did you develop your talent?" she asked.

"It just came," I said, shifting slightly in my perch on the couch, which was really hard under the velvet. "I didn't ask for it. I didn't want it. I was only eleven!"

"But you thought a lot about yourself? How you looked? What other people thought of you?" Althea asked.

"I was an actress," I said. "That was my job! It really mattered that I looked a certain way, that people liked me. The advertisers and the network people and the director and the producers and the other actors—everyone was counting on me being popular!"

I'd never quite said those words out loud before. I'm not sure I'd really understood that when I was eleven, before I'd developed my unwanted talents and heard other people talking about how much money was lost when I messed up.

"Indeed," Althea said dryly.

"But lots of actresses and people are like that—models! TV anchors! politicians! Lots of people depend on having a good image," I argued. "Lots of people make their money from being popular, and none of them hear voices the way I do."

"How can you be so sure?" Althea asked. "How would you know? How many people know about you?"

I opened my mouth, and then decided that now was likely not the best time to mention that hordes of paparazzi were probably right that moment preparing to descend on Springdale. I clamped my jaws back together.

Althea put her cup and saucer aside, back with the teapot. We stared at each other for a moment.

"You're saying that all actors and actresses—anyone in the public eye—they all get this?" I asked through gritted teeth. It crossed my mind: Even though I was just a kid, someone really should have mentioned this when I signed up for my Screen Actors Guild card.

Althea impatiently waved away my question. "No, no, this isn't that common," she said. "I'm talking about what triggers it, what makes it start—the *timing*, if you will, of when people develop their talent. If they have it. I was eighteen and vain, and *so* concerned about what all the boys in town thought of me. . . ."

I felt like Althea was talking in circles. I didn't care about hearing her story right now.

"But lots of people are vain," I argued. "Lots of teenagers. Why would some people get this when others don't?"

"Why do some people have brown eyes when others have blue?" Althea countered. "Why do some people have red hair? Why are some people seven feet tall?"

I was about to slip back into sarcasm: *Well, duh. Heredity, mostly. But scientists have mapped the whole human genome, and I've never heard of anything like* this *being on there.* Then I noticed that Althea was patting my arm. Her fingers felt dry and papery, a whisper's touch.

"You're a double legacy," she murmured. "Did you know that?"

Slowly she scooted forward and eased her body into a standing position, supporting herself by holding on to the chair's arms until she trusted her balance. She shuffled around the couch, past the huge table, and into the next room. She returned a few minutes later with a sheaf of rolled-up paper that was nearly as tall as she was. She laid it down on the table and motioned for me to join her.

"Spread it out," she ordered me. "That's a good girl."

Obediently I untied the three faded ribbons that held the paper in its tight roll, then unspooled it. I had to snag four saucers from the tea set to hold the edges down.

Unrolled, the paper proved to be an ancient, fragile drawing of a tree, with names and dates written in a spidery hand on every one of the hundreds of branches. The names Thaddeus and Lydia Clay were written on the trunk.

"Your father's line," Althea whispered, tracing a trail of branches all the way down to a tiny twig on the far right side of the tree. "And your mother's." She picked up a pointer I hadn't noticed leaning against the table, and traced a similarly remote, twisted trail on the opposite side of the tree.

At first I was horrified, thinking, *My mother and father were cousins?* But then I realized, staring at the tree, that it would have been something like fifth or sixth cousins, so distant that it wouldn't really have mattered.

Then I realized who they were both descended from. Who I was descended from, twice over.

"It *is* hereditary?" I gasped. "My—my parents had it too?"

Althea waved the pointer over the entire family tree. I thought of dowsing rods, Ouija board planchettes, other mysteriously magical objects that are all supposed to be fake.

"Some are only carriers," she whispered. "Some had such a weak form of the talent that they probably never knew. Others—"

"What was my father? What's my mother?" I asked. My mother's life was a complete unknown, but I racked my memory for hints about my father, signs that I'd missed noticing for my entire life. Was that why he'd hated crowds, why he'd chosen books over people—why he'd thrown himself into studying the obscure reaches of transcendentalism?

"Your father was the one who chose to move to Springdale, correct?" Althea said with a shrug.

"He said it was because my mother's family came from here," I whispered. Now that I was actually paying attention, that seemed like a really stupid reason to move halfway across the country. I squinted at the chart before me. "But you're saying my *father's* family came from Springdale too?"

"Your father might not have known," Althea said. "His branch of the family left Springdale right . . . here."

She plunged the pointer toward the chart at a name right above Thaddeus and Lydia Clay, several generations back from my father.

"So he knew, or he didn't know. . . . Either way, you're saying the fact that he moved us to Springdale means he could hear things? Like I do?" I was dizzy contemplating this possibility. I couldn't think straight.

"He didn't just move you to Springdale," Althea corrected me starchily. "He moved you to a Hearer's House in Springdale."

I'd never heard the term "Hearer's House" before, but I knew what it was. A house like mine.

I gaped at Althea.

"That's proof, then?" I asked. "You know for sure that my father—"

But Althea was shaking her head.

"No," she said slowly, in her whispery voice. "I know

very little about your father. I'm only speculating. Conjecturing."

My jaw dropped farther.

"But . . . but . . . you knew it was possible and you never *asked*?" I said incredulously. "The man lived right across the street!"

"We Hearers like our privacy," Althea said, a bit self-righteously. "It was his choice whether to tell, not mine to ask."

I stared into her wrinkled face, and there were still secrets hidden in her eyes, things I *knew* she still wasn't telling me. But I couldn't concentrate on that, because her face was suddenly blurry, hidden by a veil of tears. I was crying—sobbing, actually. Althea handed me a neatly folded handkerchief, but I couldn't quite figure out what to do with it.

Oh, Daddy, I thought. *Oh, Daddy. Were you like me? Why didn't you tell me, if you were? We could have commiserated. Helped each other. I would have understood you!*

But I could remember how I'd put my hands over my ears, shutting out everything he'd tried to tell me before our move to Springdale. I thought of the silence that had so often lain between us, the way he'd been the only one who'd ever broken it.

"How's that history paper going, Lindsay?"

"Fine."

"Which did you think was more interesting—the Huguenots or the other Calvinists?"

"Neither."

"Well, the transcendentalist viewpoint differs from Calvinists in that . . ."

Why hadn't he ever talked to me about anything important?

Why hadn't I ever told him anything important either? Why hadn't I given him a chance to understand me?

Althea gently eased the handkerchief out of my hands and wiped my wet face with it.

"I'm guessing your father had a very mild version of Hearing. Or he was very brave," Althea said. "As a professor, meeting hundreds of students every year, any one of them capable of talking about him at any moment for the rest of his life . . ."

"Brave" is not a word I ever would have connected with my father. Mousy, yes. Timid. And odd, out-of-step, embarrassing, old-fashioned, socially inept . . .

But, oh, who was I to judge?

I blinked back the tears, trying to focus my eyes on Althea's face, trying to fix my mind on my memory of Dad. It was threatening to become the memory of somebody else—somebody brave. And I couldn't have that. I couldn't bear to think about how much more that meant I'd lost when I'd shut my father out, when I'd stopped listening to him, when I'd spent five years being mad at him before he was gone forever.

But I did what you told me to do, Daddy, I wanted to protest. *I studied so hard! Why didn't you ever want me to do anything more . . . personal?*

It was almost as if we'd abandoned each other, just not as thoroughly as my mother had.

My mother . . .

"What about . . . ," I began. But my body betrayed me: I had to stop to sniff and gulp. My acting ability abandoned me too—it was all I could do just to get the words out. "What about my mother?"

With a shaking hand I pointed to the spot on the far left side of the tree chart, where her name stood out on one of the highest twigs. Elaine Stone. "Curran" was written after the "Stone" in slightly less-faded ink. For the first time I noticed that there was a small red dot beside her name. I stepped back, and suddenly I saw red dots all over the place, beside practically every name at the top of the chart.

"What's that mean?" I asked, touching the dot with my finger.

"Those of us who stayed or moved back to Springdale, the ones who live in the houses our ancestors built, most of us do fine," Althea said. "The others . . ."

"What?" I demanded. "What happens to them?"

Althea pressed her lips together. Shaking her head, she backed away from the table.

"No," she said. "No. You aren't ready to hear this."

"Please!" I begged. "I am! Tell me! You talked to my mother, didn't you? I couldn't hear you, but I could hear her, and Mrs. Mullin said it was you she was talking to—where is she? Why couldn't I hear you?"

Althea had backed up almost to the wall. I felt like a bully, yelling at this fragile old woman, cornering her in her own house.

"The houses work in both directions," she muttered. "Inside, we can't hear people outside. And people outside can't hear us."

"Totally soundproofed," I said.

Althea's fingers brushed a black contraption on a shelf built into the wall. It took me a minute to realize what it was: a telephone, one so ancient-looking that Alexander Graham Bell himself might have once used it.

"You called my mother, didn't you?" I asked. "You were standing right there and you called her." I could hear my mother's voice in my head again, but only as a memory. *Yes, I have a daughter. I used to have a daughter. My Lindsay . . .* "Where was she?"

Althea didn't answer. I towered over her, a giantess defeated by a dwarf. I drew back my hand and hit the wall.

"What is it about these houses, anyway?" I asked, my voice raspy now. "What makes them so special?"

"I don't know," Althea murmured. "Our ancestor's secrets were lost. That's why no one can build any more. That's why no one can leave."

I could see what must have happened. My mother or her parents or her grandparents had left Springdale. They probably hadn't even known the secret lurking in their genetic code. Probably no one had known until my mother . . . what? What had happened to her?

I hit the wall again, harder this time.

"You have to tell me about my mother!" I yelled.

Althea peered up at me, uncowed.

"I won't," she said, steel in her voice.

"Then I . . . I'll . . ." I cast about for the most appalling threat I could think of. I'd learned my negotiating skills in Hollywood. If you wanted something right away, you hit people where it hurt; you threatened the very thing they valued most. I knew just what it was with Althea, because she was like me. "I'll talk about you all the time," I said. "I'll stand out in my backyard and babble, 'Althea, Althea, Althea . . .' Anytime you leave your house, you'll hear me."

Althea lifted her head even higher.

"Go right ahead," she said. "Be my guest. But you should know, child"—she laughed, a sound like tinkling chimes, or breaking glass—"I haven't left this house in sixty years."

My head jolted forward, thudding against the wall. *Sixty years. Sixty years. More than three times as long as I've been alive.* Suddenly I saw how it was. Everything I thought I knew about Springdale—all those jaunty college students, the cheers coming from the football stadium, the parents driving in with their minivans and SUVs to pick up and drop off their kids before and after every break—it was all a cover. Even my father and Mrs. Mullin—they were anomalies. The real Springdale was people like Althea Gooding, cowering alone in crumbling old houses, hiding out from everything they didn't want to hear. How many Altheas were there in Springdale? Ten? Twenty? A hundred?

Was I an Althea too?

Althea's face softened. Her eyes grew a little misty.

"Look," she said. "You have a safe house. You stay there. You'll be fine."

"No," I said. "No. I can't!"

And I wasn't even sure what I meant. Was I protesting because of what Roz knew, and how easily she could tell? And because, if she told anyone, my house would stop being safe?

Or did I just not want to be another Althea?

"Of course you can," Althea said gently.

She was smiling now, but it was a horror-movie smile, a creepy fairy-tale smile, the sweet old lady who'd offered candy suddenly revealed as a wicked witch. Only, this wicked witch didn't want to shove me into a fiery oven. She wanted me buried alive.

I whirled around and ran.

Chapter 26

It was a straight shot from Althea Gooding's house to my own, but somehow I got lost. Don't ask me how that happened. Maybe I stumbled off the sidewalk into the unfenced grass, across dozens of neighbors' yards; maybe I was so blinded by tears that I dashed right past my own front door. Between running and gasping and sobbing and—I think—screaming, too, I wasn't aware of anything around me until suddenly I found myself on an unfamiliar street, and I heard a voice holler, "Dude! Don't you have a three o'clock class?"

A boy coming toward me flipped open a cell phone to check the time, and then flicked his hair back—a surfer's move, hundreds of miles away from any ocean. He grinned, shrugged, and said, "Can't get there in two minutes. Guess I'm not going today. Oh, well."

Three o'clock, I thought, panicked. *Three o'clock. Two minutes till three o'clock.* I peered around, looking for some familiar sight, some clue that could point my way home in two minutes or less. There was a green street sign at the end of the block, and I ran toward it.

CLAY STREET it said, in formal lettering. *Oh, probably named for Thaddeus Clay,* I realized. *Thanks a lot, buddy. You and your search for God. How hard were you really trying?*

I didn't have time to indulge my anger with my long-dead ancestor. I squinted hard, trying instead to remember if I'd ever seen Clay Street marked on a map, or glowing in the outlines of Google Earth. I craned my neck, looking down the cross street at unfamiliar tiny houses, unfamiliar tiny yards. Some of them looked a lot like my house and my yard, and somehow that made it seem even worse that I was lost. It was like thinking you recognized someone you loved in a roomful of strangers, running up to him in joy and relief—and then, when you got close, discovering that that person was a stranger too.

It's three o'clock! Oh—there's my girl, the prisoner in Iowa said, his voice joining a sudden rising tide of chatter in my mind.

"No!" I shouted.

Desperately I ran toward the nearest house that resembled mine. The psychology types might have said this was transference, but I had a sudden idea, a sudden hope. I jumped up onto the doorstep, pressed my body as close as I could to the door . . .

Oh, please, oh, please, oh . . . yes!

Silence. This was another safe house.

I grinned, delighted with myself, delighted with the success of my wild guess. I spun around, because I had the notion that it would be better to keep the back of my head, rather than the front, pressed as close as possible to the house's safety.

The surfer dude wannabe and his friend were standing in the yard, staring at me.

"Are you . . . ," surfer dude began.

"All right?" his friend finished.

I visualized myself as a Springdale College sorority girl, the kind who cracked her gum and blew bubbles.

"Oh, sure," I said, shrugging without moving my head from the wood door. "Drama class homework, you know?"

"Oh," surfer dude said. "If you say so."

They walked on, but kept giving me pointed glances over their shoulders.

I realized I'd had my arms spread out, like I was trying to hug the house, and now more like I was trying to guard it. Several more clumps of kids were approaching, probably other college students coming back from classes or work or whatever. I decided to go for a less conspicuous pose. Carefully, making sure I didn't lean too far forward, I slid down into a sitting position, my legs dangling over the edge of the doorstep. I tilted my head back, impersonating a lazy, carefree coed trying to get some sun on her face.

Now—I peeked—none of the kids walking by gave me

a second glance. I had silence and safety, and nobody was going to bother me.

But the problem with silence was, then I could hear my own thoughts.

Sixty years in the same house . . . Why wouldn't she tell me about my mother? . . . Why did Mrs. Mullin act like talking to Althea Gooding would be the answer to all my problems?

Then I understood. I slid slightly forward, until I was pretty sure that my mouth would be outside the house's protection, even though my brain wasn't.

"That was really mean, Mrs. Mullin," I muttered, hoping that she'd be able to hear me. It was three o'clock; I couldn't quite remember what day of the week it was, but maybe she'd be at work. And I knew the English department building at the college didn't provide any protection. "You should have at least warned me what Althea was like."

I felt like Ebenezer Scrooge, being forced to see all those visions. Althea Gooding was my Ghost of Christmas Future, the one horror I should still be able to prevent. Sixty years in the same house, and I'd be just like Althea.

What if I stayed in the same house for just fifty-nine years? Or . . . thirty? It didn't matter. Any amount of time—any portion of my life spent cowering in my home like Althea— would be wasted.

"All right! All right! I'll admit—she got to me, just like you wanted her to," I muttered. "But what good does that do? I still have just as many problems as before. More." I realized that Mrs. Mullin might not be able to hear me now, because I was talking about myself, not her. "I thought you said you wanted to help me."

I couldn't resist: I dipped my head a little forward.

I heard the prisoner in Iowa say, . . . *hug her . . . kiss her . . . .* and a second grader in New Mexico say, *I don't care if they're out of style now. I want shoes like hers!* And dimly, under the tidal wave of other chatter, I thought I also heard Mrs. Mullin whisper, *You're not the easiest person to help, you know? I'm doing the best I can.*

I smiled. This may have been the very first moment in five years that I'd truly appreciated my talent. It was actually kind of . . . charming, to be able to talk back and forth with Mrs. Mullin like this.

"Yeah, well, what I need is help with a media disaster," I said. "Because that's what's coming for me. I need a good PR firm. I need a good spokesman. I need someone who can make this all go away, who can keep me safe forever . . . without having me turn into Althea Gooding."

I leaned forward again, listening once more. I heard what seemed to be the whole world talking in my head—the whole world except Mrs. Mullin. My smile faded.

She wouldn't have heard me. She wouldn't have heard anything I'd said, because I'd been thinking and talking only about myself.

"Um, hello?" someone said.

It took me a moment to realize that the voice came from right in front of me, from a voice box and mouth and lips that were physically present. I looked up to see a young couple standing before me, the woman clutching the man's hand like she didn't quite trust him not to wander away.

"This is *our* house," the woman said accusingly.

I jumped up, murmuring, "Oh, sorry. I didn't know."

The woman was glaring at me—like I was some siren, intent on luring her boyfriend or husband away. But I couldn't quite bring myself to dive completely out of the house's protection right away. And I wondered . . .

"So, like, have you lived here for very long?" I asked, trying to sound like a spacey high school student, the kind who would believe urban myths. "Like, I've heard rumors about this house, not like it's haunted or anything, but, like, if you live here, you develop special talents or something."

"I can whistle 'The Star-Spangled Banner,'" the man offered, sounding amused.

The woman whirled on him.

"You're tone-deaf," she said. "You can't even sing."

"Well, like, maybe it's more that, if you live here, the house blocks things," I said, forging on even though the woman's glare was deepening. "Like, maybe if you're inside the house, you can't hear him sing."

I put on an amiable grin, pretending to be so stupid that I didn't realize the woman was annoyed. I thought I'd given pretty good clues. If they didn't know how special their house was, I hadn't given anything away. But if either of these people was like me and Mrs. Mullin and Althea, they'd react. The man, I thought, would probably wink at me; the woman would just widen her eyes and then, a moment later, say craftily,

"Now that you mention it, I do remember hearing a few stories . . ."

Neither of them did anything.

After a few moments the woman stepped up onto the doorstep, all but knocking me off.

"Do you *mind?*" she said rudely, shoving her key into the lock. "This house doesn't even have a decent water heater, it's got no insulation, the wind comes right in through the walls—believe me, it's nothing special. It should have been torn down years ago. It's a pit!"

She jerked the door open and stormed inside.

"Sorry," the man said to me, wincing. "She lost out on a grant today. She's kind of in a bad mood. . . . You should probably leave."

This wasn't my house, and the angry woman made it a slightly dangerous place. But I still hovered at the edge of its protection.

"Can you tell me how to get to Vine Street from here?" I asked plaintively. "I got a little turned around."

"Four blocks that way," the man said, pointing.

"Roger!" the woman screamed from inside.

"Better go," the man said.

He went inside, and I inched along the wall, hunched over so they couldn't see me through any windows. I could hear them fighting already.

"You act like you don't even care!"

"Well, if you wouldn't . . ."

At the corner of the house I looked ahead. The next house was a 1970s-style ranch. I ran right past it to the edge of the old house after that. *Ah, safe again.* Three more houses. *Safe again.* And then, four safe houses in a row . . .

I was working on a plan in my mind. *When the paparazzi come to my house, I will sneak out. Maybe Mrs. Mullin will let me stay with her while I'm trying to buy one of these other houses. . . . If some of the people who live here don't even appreciate them, it shouldn't be very hard.* But I was already forgetting the frightening vision of myself turning into Althea Gooding. It was hard to make plans when I had opposite goals, one side of my brain screaming, *Hide! Hide!* while the other was countering, *No, you can't! You can't live your whole life like that!*

I turned the corner back to my street, racing from house to house so quickly that I caught only snippets of words in between safe zones. And then there was my own house up ahead, completely familiar, but completely temporary. It probably wouldn't be able to provide its protection to me much longer than all those other houses I'd just zipped past.

No, scratch that. Its protection has already expired.

Roz was sitting on the front step.

Chapter 27

She'd already seen me by the time I saw her, so I couldn't even whirl around and run away again. She was the type who would chase me down.

And I'd bet she was a faster runner.

I opted for surliness as my best defense. If I couldn't escape, at least I could make her feel guilty.

"What? Are they going to hand you the check directly?" I asked as I slowed to a stroll, up my sidewalk. "Right in front of me?"

I leaned in close enough to the house so that nobody else was talking in my brain while I scowled at Roz.

She stared up at me, bafflement written across her face.

"What?" she said.

"You probably think it's like being a bounty hunter. You have to be right there, actively shoving the fugitive back into captivity," I sneered. "Or like slave hunters, picking escapees off the Underground Railroad. Aren't you just the tiniest bit afraid that the tabloids won't pay like they promised? How much did you sell me out for, anyhow?"

"Sell you out . . . ?" Roz repeated blankly. Then something changed in her expression. She drew in her next breath as though she had knives poking into her lungs. "You think I called a news conference or something? You think I'd do that to you?"

"Didn't you?" I asked mockingly. But my voice faltered; I couldn't quite stay in character while I was staring her in the eye. *She* wasn't playing the right role. She was staring right back at me, not bowing her head in shame.

"Lindsay, I haven't told anyone about . . . what I heard," Roz said.

"You didn't?" I asked. I stumbled forward and sank down on the doorstep beside her. "You really didn't?"

She shook her head.

"Even if I wanted to, who'd believe me?" she asked, grinning slightly. Her eyes were wide and sympathetic—she was so clearly innocent that my paranoia slipped away. This was *Roz*. She wasn't my enemy. She wouldn't tell. She'd watch out for me as much as she did for all the other needy people she knew.

"I didn't think of that," I muttered. "I guess I just forgot . . . how it would sound to someone who didn't know."

I put my hands down on the concrete step, and it felt so firm and safe beneath my fingers. My house was completely safe again—it had never stopped being safe. There was no reason I couldn't step back inside, shut the door on the rest of the world, and just savor my own peace and quiet.

Except that, if I did that, I would be another Althea Gooding, hiding out, cowering alone in a little box. "I haven't left this house in sixty years." I couldn't get the sound of her voice out of my mind.

I sighed and let go of the doorstep. I lifted my hands and dropped my head down against them, my face resting on my fingertips.

"I'm not sure I understand," Roz said gently. "What I heard you and Mrs. Mullin talking about—it's not really possible. Is it? Mrs. Mullin made it sound like she could hear you and Toby talking in Chicago, when she was standing in her own backyard. And you both made it sound like you could hear all sorts of things . . . people talking about you. Did I miss something? Did you guys just bug each other's phones? Are you part of some psycho spy ring, like in the movies?"

I could act my way out of this, I thought. *I know how to lie.* I raised my head slightly and peeked over at Roz through my fingers. There was something in her expression that made me think she kind of wanted to be lied to. It would be easier for both of us.

But I opened my mouth and . . . I couldn't do it. The lies I was planning, the glib jokes I thought I'd make to wash away her suspicions—all of it died on my tongue.

"It's true," I said abruptly. "No electronics involved. I don't know about Mrs. Mullin, but ever since I was eleven,

I've been able to hear every single thing anybody says about me, no matter where they are."

Roz winced.

"Lindsay, that's . . . Hearing voices is like . . . mental illness. Schizophrenia, I think. There's medicine that could help you, that could make the voices go away. Make you feel better."

This was what she'd come back to tell me. Once again, she was trying to take care of someone in need.

I remembered that I'd just been running around Springdale like a madwoman, screaming and getting lost. And then I'd crept back home by lurking under strangers' windowsills, hugging the corners of their houses before fleeing to the edge of the next house. I'm sure all of that would have looked crazy to anyone who'd seen me. And I didn't need to look in a mirror to know that my hair was tangled, my clothing disheveled, my face flushed and sweaty.

Still, I turned and faced Roz squarely.

"I'm not crazy," I told her. "The voices are real."

Roz toyed with a thread unraveling from the right knee of her jeans. She gazed at me sympathetically.

"Well, of course, it would *seem* that way to you," she said. "Did you ever see the movie *A Beautiful Mind*? We watched it in psychology class. This guy completely imagined a friend, and the friend's little girl, and all sorts of conversations with them. And none of it was real, but to him—"

"No," I interrupted. "Listen." I swallowed hard. Did I really want to do this? I did. "When Toby and Darnell came to your restaurant—Straley's?—to tell you that they'd kidnapped me, the three of you sat in a back booth. And when they'd explained what they'd done, you said, 'Ah, guys, were you thinking they'd give out a Stupidest Move of the Year prize at the end of school? And did you think that it'd be a good thing to win it?'"

Roz's expression didn't change.

"Toby could have told you that," she said.

"But Toby didn't hear what you said when you went back into the kitchen and asked your boss if you could leave early," I said. "I don't remember it all word for word, but you told her something like, 'You won't believe what those boys have done this time. Do you know a good lawyer?' And she said, 'What is it now?' And you said, 'Toby and Darnell saw some girl over in Springdale they think is Lindsay Scott. Remember, that child actress from, like, five or six years ago?' And she said, 'Oh, yeah, my granddaughter Elisha had a Lindsay Scott lunch box.' And you said, 'Well, instead of just asking for her autograph, like any normal stalker would do, Toby and Darnell decided she needed to be "rescued," except it probably seemed more like a kidnapping to her. So they took her out to the Party Barn in McGonigle and just left her there. And she's probably run away by now, or called the cops, but—'"

"Stop!" Roz said. "How could you know all that?" Her eyes darted about; she seemed to be looking everywhere at once for a logical explanation. "You talked to Terry, didn't you?"

"Terry's your boss?"

Roz nodded, just once, down then up. She looked afraid to move any more than that. Maybe I had managed to repeat it all, word for word. Or close enough.

I dug into the pocket of my pants, pulled out the cell phone I'd bought to have a Chicago area code to fool Mrs. Mullin's husband with. I held out the phone to Roz.

"Here," I said. "Call her yourself and find out. Or—" I remembered something else I could use, something I hadn't really even paid attention to at the time. "Or you could call your little sister. Ask her if I've ever talked to *her*. Remember that night I went to Chicago? That same night, about midnight, your sister got up to get a drink of water, and you were still up doing homework, and she told you she'd been dreaming about becoming a famous actress, and that was what she wanted to do. And then you said something like, 'I don't know, Charity. I met someone who's an actress, and it seems like it kind of messed her up.' And then I think you must have felt bad about discouraging her, because then you said of course *she* wouldn't get messed up. *She* had a good head on her shoulders."

Roz's face was completely pale now. She didn't reach for the phone.

"There's no way you could know all that," she said.

I shrugged, like someone being falsely modest.

"You didn't just know what we said," Roz said. "You knew where we were when we said it."

"Oh, yeah." This time my shrug was truly dismissive. "Sometimes I can do that, too."

I realized that was why I thought Roz probably lived in a trailer: I'd seen it in my mind, picturing her discussion with her little sister. I had a vague sense of extreme cleanliness, of cheap linoleum that had still been polished to a shine. And I thought Roz's little sister had been wearing a nightgown covered in balloon-faced Care Bears.

I didn't tell Roz that. I didn't want to completely freak her out.

"Then—then you and Mrs. Mullin should be spies," she said, a little of the color coming back into her face. "Why aren't you guys working for the CIA?"

"I only hear what people say about me. And sometimes just a little bit of the conversation before and after," I said. "As far as I know, Mrs. Mullin only hears things people say about *her*. Knowing about our own lives, gossip about ourselves—it wouldn't really help national security."

Roz dipped her head down.

"But then you know all the mean things I said about you," she said. "Yesterday, when Toby told me about taking you to Chicago. I said you were using him, just taking advantage of him. I said you were inconsiderate, not even asking if he had any problems with going overnight. I said actresses only fall in love for, like, five minutes, and then they shove one guy aside for the next guy. . . ."

I started laughing.

"Roz," I said. "You told me every bit of that right to my face!"

Roz stopped in the middle of her list.

"Oh," she said, snorting. "I guess you're right."

"Did you say anything worse to him than you did to me?" I asked.

Slowly Roz shook her head.

"I was actually a little bit nicer with Toby," she admitted.

It was weird, but somehow this made it okay that Roz had said mean things about me to Toby, since she'd also said them directly to me. I admitted that I hadn't heard her talking to Toby. I explained about the safe houses, and about everything I'd found out from Mrs. Mullin and Althea Gooding. I told how maddening they'd both been, refusing to tell me everything I wanted to know, especially about my mother.

And Roz listened. Under her steady gaze, I found myself telling her things I was only beginning to realize.

"The thing that bothers me the most is that Althea knows where my mother is, but she won't tell me," I said. "Mrs. Mullin knows too. And—I never thought I even cared about my mother!" I knew as I spoke that this was a lie—acting, bravado, trying to hide again. I forced myself back to honesty. "I mean—I shouldn't care! I don't remember anything about her!"

"Oh, Lindsay," Roz said, shaking her head. A mischievous look came into her eye. "Didn't they have any therapists out there in Hollywood? It's true, my therapy's been kind of do-it-yourself, out of books and off the Internet, but haven't you ever heard of abandonment issues? My dad left when my mom was pregnant with me—when it's the father who leaves, it's possible for the parent to run away really,

really early—and I *still* used to think that it was because I was ugly, or because I wasn't smart enough, or because I spilled my Kool-Aid . . ."

"That's crazy," I said.

"Well, yeah," Roz said, shoving her hair back from her face. "But that didn't stop me from thinking it. Don't you know that losing a parent before you're ten is an excuse to have all sorts of things go wrong with you?"

"Like hearing voices?" I said, and my voice was almost teasing.

Roz regarded me seriously.

"What if you saw this as a blessing, not a curse?" she asked.

"Oh, that's easy for you to say—," I started angrily.

Roz held up her hand.

"No, no, wait. Let me explain," she said. "I'm not saying I'd want to be able to hear everything people say about me, because even if I tried to be a really, really good person, even if I tried to do everything perfectly, so I'd hear nothing but praise, there'd still be some jerk saying, 'That Roz! She's so goody-goody . . .' You just can't ever get everyone to approve of you."

I blushed, because that was actually something I'd tried to do, in the beginning, before *Just Me and the Kids* was canceled. I'd thought if I knew my lines perfectly, if I showed up for tutoring right on time, if I let the other kids get in line for lunch ahead of me, if I went out of my way to be nice to everyone—then I'd hear only nice things about myself and it wouldn't bother me anymore.

It didn't matter. I could never be good enough. And sometimes it was the being good that made people hate me more.

"But anyhow," Roz went on, "you didn't choose this ability, but you have it. So can't you make the best of it?"

I thought maybe she'd read one too many "Change your life with online therapy!" websites. I frowned at her. Roz ignored this.

"Like, why don't you stop complaining about Mrs. Mullin and Althea Gooding and just find out where your mother is on your own?" Roz suggested.

"Oh, thanks," I said sarcastically. "I never would have thought of that. Believe it or not, I have looked online. There's nothing."

I could remember the night after my father died, sitting at the computer at three a.m., trying out different search engines and sobbing out, "Mommy, where are you?"

I didn't like thinking about that.

"I don't mean online," Roz argued. "I mean, with your 'special powers.'" She grinned a little, and elbowed me in the ribs. "Positive thinking, right?"

I rolled my eyes at her.

"How come you could see where I was when I was talking with Terry and Charity and Toby and Darnell, but you couldn't see where your mom was when you heard her?" Roz asked.

"I don't know," I said. "Knowing where people are when they talk about me—it's just not always something I can do."

But, I reflected, it was something I could almost always do if I thought about it. Whenever I heard the prisoner in Iowa talking about me, I wanted to know where he was, because I didn't want him coming any closer. Knowing his location just automatically went along with hearing him.

Come to think of it, my mother was just about the *only* person I'd ever had trouble locating when I wanted to. Why was that?

"Oh! Oh! I know!" Roz was suddenly practically bouncing up and down on the step, she was so excited about her idea. "You think your mom might have the same talent you've got, right? And this afternoon for the first time ever, you figured out how to communicate in your mind with Mrs. Mullin, who also has your same talent. So if you want to know where your mom is . . . why don't you just ask her?"

Chapter 28

I stared at Roz. The idea was so obvious that I felt like a complete idiot.

"Why didn't I think of that?" I moaned.

Roz laid her hand on my back.

"Lindsay," she said very solemnly. "This is why we tell other people our problems. Because sometimes an outsider can see solutions we can't see ourselves." She dropped the solemn act and gave me a little shove. "Go ahead and try it!"

I resisted the shove. I kept my body planted firmly on the doorstep.

"What should I say?" I whimpered.

"I know this sounds really radical and bizarre, but what about, 'Hey, Mom, where are you?'" Roz suggested.

"But will she know that she has to answer in a way that

it's like she's talking about me, or I won't be able to hear her?" I asked. I was being too cautious. If Mom was like me, she'd know the rules.

"Then you add, 'And when you answer, refer to yourself as "Lindsay's mom," or I won't be able to hear you,'" Roz said impatiently. "Go!"

She gave me another shove, and this one was hard enough that I slid off the doorstep. I landed sprawled in the grass. The voices in my head seemed muted now, bearable. I opened my mouth, but somehow couldn't get beyond that.

"I—I can't," I told Roz.

"Fine. I'll do it," Roz said. She sprang up and stepped away from the house, facing me. "Lindsay's mom," she said, projecting her voice like someone onstage. "I'm seeking Lindsay's mom. Your daughter wants to know where you are. So just say, 'Lindsay, your mother is right here in . . .' well, wherever you are. Say it out loud, wherever you are, and Lindsay will hear you."

Roz looked over at me, expectantly.

And I *listened.* I listened for a voice beyond the prisoner muttering about me in Iowa, beyond the giggling kids watching *Just Me and the Kids* after school, beyond the bored pressers in a dry cleaning shop flipping through channels and making fun of me to pass the time. I listened so hard I felt like my ears turned inside out, my brain turned inside out. I imagined that I was listening the way I had once spoken, when my voice was amplified and digitized and duplicated and sent out, around the world. I was listening to every part of the world at once.

I didn't hear my mother's voice.

"Mom?" I whispered. "Please talk to me?"

Still nothing.

Tears pricked at my eyes, and I was suddenly mad at myself. My mother hadn't talked to me in sixteen years. Why would she bother talking to me now?

Roz flopped down in the grass beside me.

"Sorry," she said. "I just thought . . . It *seemed* like such a great idea."

"So did you ever go chasing after your dad like that?" I asked angrily. "Did you have a nice reunion with him?"

Roz shook her head.

"No. He pretty much drank himself to death when I was two, so I missed out on that opportunity," she said. "No amount of being pretty or smart or nice or not spilling Kool-Aid could fix that situation."

I thought about how she watched out for Toby and Darnell and her little sister, and how, since I'd met her, she'd done everything she could to watch out for me.

"You sure you're not still trying?" I asked tremulously.

Roz gave me a playful punch on the arm.

"Hey," she said. "Get yourself a website, and you'd be better than most of the amateur therapists I've seen online."

She eased her cell phone out of her pocket, glanced at it quickly, and frowned.

"I hate to do this to you," she said, "but I have to go. My shift at Straley's starts in fifteen minutes. I didn't think . . . Well, will you be all right alone? Do you want me to call someone to come and stay with you? Mrs. Mullin or—" She seemed to remember that I had nobody else, unless she called on Toby. Which she wouldn't want to do. "Or do you want to come into work with me? You can sit back in the kitchen. Terry might try to put you to work mashing potatoes or something, if we get too busy, but she'd pay you if she did that, and—"

"No." I shook my head. I could picture what she was suggesting, and it was a kindness. But the thought of being in that crowded restaurant kitchen, with all the clatter and clutter, was the last thing I needed right now. I'd seen it in my mind. I knew what it was like. "I'm really tired. I didn't sleep much last night and— Well, you know, it's been kind of a traumatic day. I'm just going to get something to eat and go to bed."

"You sure?" Roz asked.

"Yeah," I said, trying to make myself sound even more certain than I felt.

"Here's my cell number and the number at Straley's," Roz said. "Call me if you need anything." She scribbled down numbers on a piece of paper and shoved it into my hand. "I'll come back tomorrow."

I stepped back onto my doorstep to watch her drive away. But it felt different now, just as my house felt different when I opened the door and stepped inside. The house didn't feel so tiny and barricaded, like it was my last possible refuge. It didn't feel like the Alamo or Masada anymore.

But it wasn't the house that had changed. It was me.

I walked around looking at the old pictures of nine-teenth-century Springdale my dad had put up on the wall. I tried to see some sign in the squinty eyes and blurred faces that there were people like me in the pictures—people who had maybe worn their sunbonnets and hats a little lower on their faces to avoid being noticed and talked about, because of what they didn't want to hear. People who had perhaps built my house, and had known all sorts of secrets . . . I felt no particular jolt of recognition, but for the first time, looking at these pictures, I could tell that they had been real people, that they'd been happy and sad, they'd fallen in and out of love, they'd had longings and desires and hopes and sorrows and pain and joy . . .

My stomach began growling before I made it even half-way around the room, and I grumbled to one hearty-looking family cluster, "I bet you guys had more to eat for dinner than canned soup and soda!"

Then I thought, *Well, I could too, if I put any effort into it.*

I pulled the cell phone out of my pocket again and called my father's favorite sub shop. I ordered a large turkey sand-wich with everything on it and a large side of coleslaw and a two-liter bottle of cherry 7UP. When the food came, I spread it all out on the kitchen table, and then I lifted the sandwich, like a tribute, and said, "Dad." It was the first time since he'd died that I hadn't wanted to cry or scream at the thought of him.

As I started eating, I thought what it must have been like for him, sixteen years ago, being left with a baby when he already had problems of his own. I'd spent so much time imagining myself as other people—other "characters"—but I'd never once tried to put myself in his place. If I'd been more like Roz, always looking out for other people's needs, what could I have done for him?

Thinking about that—about how I never would get a chance, ever again, even to talk to him—made my appetite vanish, and I put the sandwich and coleslaw in the refrigerator, half eaten. But at least I'd remembered to wrap them up and put them away, which was a definite improvement over the first week or so after my father died.

I went upstairs and turned in my *Julius Caesar* and Neville Chamberlain papers by e-mail. They were well written and well researched and would seem well thought-out to my teachers. My teachers didn't need to know that the papers were only stand-ins, pale imitations of the real turmoil in my life.

I lay down on my bed, intending to think through everything I'd discovered that day. I even had lofty aspirations of making some plans, organizing my thoughts, figuring out a strategy for my life. But my eyelids slid shut, and the next thing I knew, I was waking up in darkness, surfacing from a thick, dreamless sleep. I blinked at the green numerals glowing on the clock beside my bed: 4:17 a.m. The numbers looked familiar, like I should remember them. I closed my eyes and pictured numbers glowing in red on a pickup dashboard. Two days ago, the clock in Toby's truck had said 4:17 when we'd stopped at the gas station.

And then it was only a few minutes later that I heard my mother's voice. What if there was something special about this time? What if that was why I'd never heard her before, because I was always asleep at four a.m.?

It's just a coincidence, I told myself. *Don't get your hopes up.*

But I was wide awake now. I rolled over, my feet landing on the floor. It was only two steps to the window, and then one quick shove at the window frame brought the fresh night air into my room. I scrambled out onto my balcony and went to stand in the very middle, where I could hear. Most of the words I heard were foreign, except for an exchange group of American kids at a hotel in Tokyo complaining, *Aw, they've got the same reruns here we have at home!*

I tilted my head back and addressed the stars.

"Mom? Are you there?" I murmured. "Can you hear me? Mom, this is Lindsay. I've been looking for you . . ." I pictured my words bouncing off satellites, triangulating back to Earth—to my mother's ears—like a diagram on a science website. "Mom, I've missed you."

The stars winked at me. The wind rustled the branches of the trees. And I heard my mother's voice: *Lindsay. Oh, Lindsay . . .*

It was barely more than a whisper or a sigh. But it was real. I heard it. And it was . . . anguished. It was not the sigh of a woman who'd intentionally walked away from her baby daughter sixteen years ago. It was the sigh of a woman who'd lost something precious, and was desperate to get it back.

"Mom?" I said, jerking to attention. "Mom, where are you? Oh, please, tell me where you are."

Silence. I waited. I remembered how Roz and I had agreed my mother should try to answer. I said, "Mom, say, 'Lindsay's mother is . . .' wherever you are. That way I'll be sure to hear you."

She didn't do that, but I heard her anyway. She sounded too baffled to be careful about how she spoke. Too worried.

But I don't know where I am. Can you . . . Can you find me?

Chapter 29

I tried.

"Mom, give me clues. What do you see around you? What time is it there? What's the weather like outside?"

Nothing.

"How long have you been there? Who brought you there? Do you see anyone else around you?"

Did I hear one more muffled *Lindsay*, or was it just my imagination, because I was listening so hard?

"Mom? Mom?"

I'm not sure how long I stood out there, yelling at the stars—and then at the first glimmers of dawn. I was starting to go hoarse when I saw a police car gliding down the street. He didn't have his lights or siren on, but he slowed in front of my house, turning the corner at a snail's pace. He parked on the side street and stepped out of his car, shining a small flashlight up toward my balcony.

Before the light could reach me through the tangle of tree limbs, the only area still swathed in darkness, I scrambled backward through the window and pulled it firmly shut behind me. I pressed back against the wall, out of sight, and hoped he hadn't detected the motion.

Who called the cops? Who? I wondered. *Come on, people. I wasn't anywhere near as loud as a frat party!*

But I tried to figure out who'd seen or heard me. Was it Althea Gooding? Was it the same neighbor who'd been quoted in that tabloid article Toby and Darnell saw? And that cop down there—was he the same one who'd told me my father was dead?

I could imagine how I'd looked, standing out on my balcony, screaming at the sky.

The doorbell rang.

Answer it? Don't answer it?

I decided this wasn't something I could hide from. I belted a robe around my waist and walked downstairs. I opened the door slowly, yawning.

"I'm sorry to bother you, miss," the police officer—a different one, fortunately—said. "But there was a report of a disturbance at your house, and I saw the lights on . . ."

Oops. I'd forgotten to turn out the downstairs lights when I'd gone to bed the night before.

I yawned again, maybe a little too dramatically.

"That's okay," I said, clearing my throat, trying to cover up the hoarseness. "I was already up. I was doing my morning tai chi out on my balcony." I hoped that the police officer knew enough about tai chi that he wouldn't be surprised that I'd been outside flailing my arms at the sky—but not so much that he would have expected me to have done it silently.

His expression changed.

"Oh, tai chi! That explains it." Maybe he wasn't totally convinced. He glanced quickly behind me. "So you're sure nothing's wrong?"

Should I say that my mother was missing and even she didn't know where she was? Should I say that I suspected that she'd been kidnapped, or co-opted into a secret government program like the kind Roz had suggested?

Did I want to ensure that the police officer thought I was crazy?

"Really," I said, smiling. "Everything's fine."

"Glad to hear it," the officer said, smiling back. "Just let us know if that changes, all right?"

When I shut the door behind the police officer—after his third apology for bothering me—I wished I could shut out a few questions along with him. How much had my neighbors heard? How much did the cops know? Where was my mother? How could she not know where she was?

I stared out the front window at Althea Gooding's house—her porch light glowing softly through the first rays of dawn, her windows blank and shadowed. I considered stalking across the street, pounding on her door until I got an answer. But I was a little scared that once I started pounding on her door, I wouldn't be able to stop. I could see how it would sound in the *Springdale Messenger*: "Teen arrested for harassing elderly neighbor."

I reached for the phone instead.

"Mrs. Mullin, please wake up," I babbled into an answering machine. "You've got to tell me more. I've been talking to my mother, but that's not enough. I have to have answers! Please, please answer the phone!"

Was I crying? Was I putting on an act? No, I didn't need to. My anguish was real.

The phone clicked, and I jumped.

"You've progressed much faster than I expected," Mrs. Mullin said on the other end of the line.

"Progressed?" I said. "*Progressed?* What does that mean?"

"Teenagers are bound to change their perspective a few times as they grow," Mrs. Mullin said.

Mrs. Mullin must have taken lessons in Sphinx-talk from Althea Gooding.

"Look," I said. "You've got to help me. I just want to find my mother. *She* wants me to find her."

Mrs. Mullin was silent for a long moment. I began to fear that she, like Althea Gooding, was going to tell me no. Or that she'd simply laid the phone down and walked away. But then she spoke softly: "I think we should talk about this in person. I'll be right there."

I was pacing by the time she arrived.

Mrs. Mullin was dressed up, with earrings that looked like buttons, and a spangled necklace, and a maroon dress that appeared to be more silk than polyester. She caught me staring at her outfit.

"I was just getting ready for church when you called," she explained.

"Searching for God, like your ancestors?" I said, in much too nasty a voice, considering that I wanted something from her.

But Mrs. Mullin tilted her head to the side, considering this.

"I'm not sure I have quite the same expectations," she said slowly. "Or maybe I'm just not as certain that I'll always understand what I find?"

"But you go to church."

"Yes," she said. "I go to church. Faithfully, you might say. What I find there is important to me."

This wasn't what I wanted to talk about, but I could see a segue.

"So you want to help people," I said. "All that 'love your neighbor as yourself' stuff." I'd done a religious studies course online. "So you'll help me find my mother."

Mrs. Mullin sighed heavily.

"I'm not sure you're ready to hear this," she said. "The last time I told you anything, you started hyperventilating."

"I'm *ready*!" I said impatiently. "It's more like I'm going to hyperventilate if you *don't* tell me!"

Mrs. Mullin regarded me steadily. I began to regret what I'd said—it had sounded too much like a little kid threatening to hold her breath if she didn't get what she wanted. (That had happened more than once in *Just Me and the Kids* episodes.) I stood up taller, trying to look mature and responsible, able to take startling news like an adult.

Mrs. Mullin sighed again. "Perhaps we should sit down," she said.

"Fine," I said. "Be my guest."

I waved my hand toward my father's chair, indicating she could sit there.

"You too," Mrs. Mullin said.

I pulled a chair over from the kitchen table and slid into it. Mrs. Mullin watched me.

"None of this is simple," she said. "You have to understand, I came into my 'gift' late in life. I didn't start hearing other people's opinions of me until I went through menopause."

I made a face—who wants to hear about menopause?— but I pretended that I was only impatient.

"What's that got to do with my mother?" I asked.

"I'm working up to that," Mrs. Mullin said. She fingered one of the strands of her necklace. It was spiky and studded with maroon-colored glass. "I'm just trying to tell you that I'd already formed my opinions of the world before this came to me. I already knew who my friends and enemies were, who I could trust and who I couldn't. I knew . . ." She hesitated for a moment, and then went on. "I knew what was crazy and what wasn't."

I thought I could hurry her along.

"So you thought people who heard voices were crazy,

until you started hearing voices yourself," I said. "And then you changed your mind."

Mrs. Mullin dropped the strand of necklace and crossed her arms over her stomach.

"Not exactly," she said. "I'm still not convinced that it isn't craziness, what you and I can do."

"It'd be crazy if we imagined everything," I countered. "But what we hear—it's *true*. It's accurate. It's like—people thought Galileo was crazy, for saying the earth rotated around the sun instead of the other way around. And Christopher Columbus—some people thought he was crazy for believing that the earth was round. But Galileo, Columbus—they were *right*. They were informed, and the people who thought they were crazy were just ignorant."

These were new thoughts I was expressing. I'd never before seen myself as a visionary, a voice for truth in a crazy world, like Galileo or Columbus. I remembered Roz's gentle suggestion, after telling me I could have schizophrenia: "There's medicine that could help you, that could make the voices go away. Make you feel better."

"There's plenty of ignorance to go around," Mrs. Mullin said, pursing her lips slightly.

I was out of patience.

"So where's my mother?" I demanded.

Mrs. Mullin gazed at me sadly. She shifted in her chair, leaning forward like she was about to reach out to me.

"Oh, Lindsay, can't you guess?" she said. "She's in a mental hospital."

Chapter 30

I should have guessed, but I hadn't. Those two words, "mental hospital," hit me like a slap in the face. I was very careful not to recoil. *Thank you very much, Olivia Jerome, for the acting lessons on how to hide pain.*

"But she's not crazy," I said immediately, almost reflexively. "She's just . . . gifted. Like you and me. Right?"

Mrs. Mullin raised an eyebrow. "And by not crazy, you mean . . . ?"

"I mean, she doesn't hear any voices that aren't real." I was firm in my definition. "She's not . . . delusional."

Mrs. Mullin smoothed the silky maroon skirt clumped in her lap. She erased all the wrinkles before answering.

"Real or not, you and I both know the voices are distracting," she said. "Difficult to deal with. You want to define craziness as hearing and believing things that aren't real. What if the definition is really based on what you do with what you hear and believe? Whether you can function in spite of—or because of—those things?"

Mrs. Mullin was so earnest. For a second I could imagine her standing at the front of a class, a very wise college professor, instead of being the person who made sure there was enough toilet paper in the English department bathroom.

"So you're sane because you can function properly," I said, and there was a bitter twist to my words. "And the rest of us . . . ?"

Mrs. Mullin bunched up the silk she'd just smoothed, clutching it in her hands.

"I haven't made a study of it, the way Althea Gooding has," she admitted. "But from what she says, everyone in Springdale who has access to a safe house, a refuge from the voices every now and then—all of us manage to stay on the sane side of the equation."

"You're calling Althea Gooding sane?" I asked in disbelief. I was going to say, *And me?*

"In her own way, yes," Mrs. Mullin said. "She watches out for everyone else."

"How can she watch out for anyone?" I protested. "She hasn't left her house in sixty years!"

Mrs. Mullin pantomimed dialing a phone, lifting a receiver to her ear.

"She spends hours every day on the phone," she said. "She's got her—what do the cell phone commercials call it?—her *network*. She's figured out what works for her. She takes care of everyone who Hears."

I couldn't help it: I was already revising my viewpoint

of Althea Gooding. My memories of her house instantly seemed less museum-like and dusty.

"Althea's choice wouldn't have been right for me," Mrs. Mullin continued. "But I can respect it. Given the chance to totally fixate on what other people said about her, she turned her back on all of it—but not on the people. It's like . . . like knowing someone who's Amish. I can respect them doing all that hard work by hand, but I don't see any reason to give up electricity myself."

This annoyed me, Mrs. Mullin expecting me to see complexity and nuance like that, when I'd just been hit with such a shocking revelation.

"I thought you wanted me to meet her to see what I *shouldn't* be like," I complained.

Mrs. Mullin raised an eyebrow.

"Maybe I did," she said. "Would that be the right thing for you to do? When the job of taking care of all the Hearers in Springdale is already taken?"

I stifled the impulse to grab Mrs. Mullin by the shoulders of her silky dress and shake her back and forth until she could talk to me without sounding so condescending.

"So was Althea Gooding taking care of my mother when she called her?" I asked sarcastically.

Mrs. Mullin grimaced.

"Once a Hearer has been institutionalized," she said, her voice suddenly too careful, all the emotions blocked, "and they're on antipsychotic drugs . . . Well, did you ever try drugs or alcohol to deal with the voices?"

I hit the side of my chair.

"What is it with everyone thinking that, just because I was an actress—?"

Mrs. Mullin held up her hands, apologetically.

"It's a fairly common response," she said. "Even for *ordinary* people." Was she making fun of me? If so, the mirth was quickly gone. "But it's a very, very bad idea. Drugs—including prescription ones—only make things worse."

The grimness in her voice made me shiver.

"Then why aren't you out there telling people that?" I said accusingly. "Telling doctors, telling hospitals, telling what's really wrong with some of their patients? Why isn't Althea telling them, if she's so great at taking care of everyone?"

"Do you think it would do any good?" Mrs. Mullin said. "Coming from a woman who hasn't left her house in sixty years? Or coming from a secretary with only a high school education? Talking about people we've never met, who just happen to be third or fourth cousins?"

I slumped in my chair.

"You'd sound completely crazy," I whispered. "They'd put you on the drugs too."

Mrs. Mullin nodded.

"Sometimes Althea manages to convince an overnight worker, who's half asleep anyway—and not watched so carefully—to let her talk to an institutionalized Hearer just as the patient's medication is wearing off, right before the next dose. Sometimes she manages to get through," she said. "A little bit."

"And that's how I heard her talking to my mom," I muttered. "At four seventeen a.m." A new thought struck me, and I gasped. "Is my mother in a mental hospital here in Springdale?"

That would be too cruel, if my mother had been so close by for the past five years and I hadn't even known it.

But Mrs. Mullin was already shaking her head.

"Springdale doesn't have any mental hospitals," she said. "She's in California. It was two seventeen a.m. her time."

"Why doesn't she have a safe house in Springdale too?" I asked.

"She does," Mrs. Mullin said grimly. "We're sitting in it." She tapped her foot lightly against the floor of my house. "Didn't you wonder why the house wasn't included in the list of possessions you inherited from your father?"

No, I hadn't thought to wonder about that. Lists like that had made my eyes blur over. I hadn't looked at any of them very closely.

I squinted at Mrs. Mullin, trying to get my brain to function properly.

"I don't understand," I said. "If she's got this safe house, if people who live in safe houses stay sane—or sane *enough*—then why isn't my mother here now? Being sane and . . . and . . . taking care of me?" Those last four words just slipped out.

Mrs. Mullin was watching me carefully now. I sat up straight and tried to hide the anguish I'm sure had shown through on my face. I wanted Mrs. Mullin to think she could tell me anything. I wanted her to think I could take it.

Mrs. Mullin sighed.

"Perhaps you noticed that Springdale isn't the most exciting place to live," she said.

"Oh, I don't know," I said. "It has people with strange talents, *houses* with strange talents . . ."

Mrs. Mullin actually cracked a smile at that.

"True," she said. "And its very own Hollywood actress."

I rolled my eyes. Mrs. Mullin was definitely making fun of me now, but somehow I didn't mind.

She didn't dwell on any of it.

"But most people who are born and raised here—they reach a point where they think they've outgrown Springdale," she said. "They want to see the 'real' world. They want fame, fortune, excitement. Opportunity. They want to live somewhere that hasn't been in decline for the past one hundred and fifty years."

"But if my mother was already hearing voices—," I objected.

Mrs. Mullin shook her head.

"Your mother didn't grow up here," she said. "It was her parents who left. As near as Althea Gooding could tell, they weren't Hearers, so they didn't know what they were leaving, or the risks they were taking for future generations."

I was starting to get the picture.

"Why didn't someone tell them?" I asked. "Why isn't there some, I don't know, reverse welcome wagon for people leaving Springdale? Someone to go out and warn people about what might happen if they go away?"

Mrs. Mullin frowned at me, but it was a sympathetic frown this time.

"Who'd believe it?" she asked. "And why risk revealing ourselves when the odds are that the people who leave won't develop any talents at all?"

She shifted in her chair as if she were getting ready to leave. I put my hand out to stop her.

"So, okay, whatever. Why can't I bring my mother here *now*?" I said. "Can't the safe house heal her now?" I felt a flash of anger, thinking everything through. "Why didn't my dad bring her here? Why didn't you and Althea Gooding tell him to do it?" Why was I the one who had to figure everything out?

Mrs. Mullin tilted her head, regarding me sadly.

"It just doesn't work that way," she said. "Once somebody's that far gone . . . Once they themselves start believing that they're crazy . . . Once they've had judges committing them to the mental health system and they're on the drugs . . . we just can't get them back. Believe me, it's been tried. If we'd known your mother was out there, we would have tried to intervene years ago, when she first began showing symptoms, before she was so far gone. But it's too late now."

I drew myself up to my full height. My anger made me strong. I understood now what Roz had meant when she said scar tissue held her up. But it wasn't just anger and pain that fueled me. It was hope.

"Haven't you ever read any supermarket tabloids?" I asked. "It's never too late for a Hollywood actress."

Chapter 31

Mrs. Mullin didn't look impressed.

"Lindsay," she said. "We're talking about rescuing someone who's been on antipsychotic drugs for sixteen years. Not about some actress making a comeback on *Dancing with the Stars*."

I guessed Mrs. Mullin had read a few supermarket tabloids in her day.

"I have money," I said. "And connections. I can start, like, a PR campaign. People would picket the mental hospital, I bet. They'd carry signs: 'Free Lindsay's mom!'"

"And they'd talk about you," Mrs. Mullin said quietly.

"Oh." I slumped back in my chair. "Right." How could I have forgotten about that? Of course they'd talk about me. *Did you hear? That child actress who had that nervous breakdown— her mother's crazy! She's been in a psych ward for sixteen years!*

Can you believe it? . . . I bet the kid's crazy too. Yeah, like Britney Spears. . . . Or do you think it's all a publicity stunt? . . . That's really sick, saying your mother's crazy, just so you get can some attention. . . . If I tried to rescue my mother, people would talk about me so much it'd be years before I could step foot outside my house again. I would turn into Althea Gooding after all.

"But maybe that doesn't matter," Mrs. Mullin said. "Maybe it's still worth it to you to try."

There was something extra in her voice, a certain craftiness that annoyed me. I narrowed my eyes at her.

"You've been manipulating me, haven't you?" I accused. "This whole time, you've been leading me on, leading me toward the conclusions *you* want me to make." I remembered the cryptic comment she'd made over the phone: "You've progressed much faster than I expected . . ."

"You wanted me to decide on my own that I need to rescue my mother," I said, "no matter what it means to my reputation, like *she's* more important than what I might hear. What is this—Sunday school?"

Mrs. Mullin lifted her hands, a gesture of innocence.

"Hey, it's not me setting up that choice," she said. "That's how life works. You sacrifice your own desires for someone else's needs when you care about the other person. Why do you think I'm here talking to an ungrateful, surly teenager who doesn't even like me, who's never even said thank you, even *once* . . . when I could be enjoying myself at the Straley's Family Diner breakfast buffet on my way to church?"

My eyes widened in surprise. I hadn't thought about things that way. Surely I'd said thank you to Mrs. Mullin at some point. After the funeral, maybe, or when she dropped off that casserole or . . .

Okay. Maybe not.

I thought about saying "Thank you" right then, or "I *do* like you. You should know that," but the words would have seemed coerced and fake. Meaningless.

"I didn't know Straley's Family Diner had a breakfast buffet," I said instead.

"Only on the weekends," Mrs. Mullin said, grinning slightly. "And it's kind of bad for me to go there, because I always eat too much and get heartburn afterward. So, really, you're doing me a favor."

I felt forgiven.

"You're welcome, then," I said, grinning back. And the way Mrs. Mullin nodded, I could tell that she knew that my "You're welcome" really meant "Thank you."

Mrs. Mullin leaned forward again, balancing her elbows on her knees, cupping her chin in her hands.

"Lindsay," she said in a kind voice, "I know you think you're so special. You think what you and I can do is so amazing and unique. But really, what you're going through is not that different from what any teenager has to go through."

"What?" I exploded, our moment of understanding evaporating completely. "You think all this is just . . . *ordinary*?"

"No, no, hear me out," Mrs. Mullin said, taking a hand off her chin to wave it at me, warningly. "I wouldn't use the word 'ordinary.' But pretty much every kid, about the time they hit middle school, starts caring way too much about what other people think about them. I wasn't hearing voices then, but I can still remember knowing *exactly* what all the girls in my school thought in seventh grade when I got a new dress that was just like one of Susan Patry's. They thought I was a copycat, and they thought I was trying too hard to be popular, and they talked about me behind my back—I didn't hear any of their words, but I *knew.*" She took in what must have been a skeptical expression on my face. "I know it sounds pretty silly now, but at the time—that hurt. Bad. I cried myself to sleep at night and told my mother I was never going to school again."

I squinted at Mrs. Mullin, and for a moment I could picture it all, a girl with saddle shoes and a pinafore and braids flinging herself across a bed, wailing "Everyone hates me! I'm never going back to that place!" The image was in black and white, because I was thinking of it as a 1950s TV sitcom. I pictured a worried-looking mother coming into the room wearing a housedress and an apron and pearls, like the mothers in *Leave It to Beaver* or *Father Knows Best* or *The Adventures of Ozzie and Harriet*, all shows the producers of *Just Me and the Kids* had wanted us to watch for acting tips.

Bringing the mother into the scene made me lose any sense of compassion I was developing. At least Mrs. Mullin had had a mother to comfort her.

"So what?" I said grumpily. "You had, what, forty or fifty

girls talking about you? I hear the whole world making fun of me."

"Actually, it was probably more like only ten or fifteen," Mrs. Mullin said sheepishly. "I went to a very small school."

I rolled my eyes. It wasn't worth the effort to utter the words *"See what I mean?"*

"But it's not about the numbers," Mrs. Mullin said. "It's this: Eventually everyone has to get past that self-absorption, that sense that you're the center of the universe and it matters so much what other people think and say about you. And the way you get past that is, you start caring about everyone else, you start seeing their joys and sorrows as being every bit as important as your own. I think if you do that, the voices won't bother you so much, you won't hear them so strongly, you won't be so obsessed or feel so restricted."

I stared at Mrs. Mullin. She was gesturing broadly, waving her hands in the air, conjuring up some vision of life that seemed utterly foreign to me. My stare narrowed into a squint.

"I'm confused," I said. "First you say no one can rescue my mother; it's too late. And now you're saying—what? To rescue myself I have to rescue her? I have to care about her and put her needs ahead of my own?" I clutched the armrests of my chair, my knuckles turning white. "What are you telling me to do?"

Mrs. Mullin threw up her hands. But, strangely, it didn't look like a gesture of despair or defeat. It was more like someone passing a torch. Or giving a blessing.

"I'm not *telling* you to do anything," she said. "I honestly don't know what the right answer is. According to Althea Gooding, nobody's ever been able to save one of us who's been certified as 'crazy' in the outside world. But I'm proud of you for wanting to try to rescue your mother, and I do think it would help *you* to go in that direction. It's up to you, whether you think it's worth the risks. I'm just saying— What you said before, that you wanted your mother here, in this house, taking care of you? It almost certainly wouldn't be like that."

"What do you mean?" I said defensively. I hadn't thought Mrs. Mullin had paid such close attention to my little rant.

"I don't think your mother will ever be able to take care of you," Mrs. Mullin said, staring straight at me, in a way that made her gaze impossible to dodge. "I think it would always be you taking care of her."

Chapter 32

Mrs. Mullin left.

Everything we said after her little pronouncement seemed anticlimactic, unimportant, even when I grabbed her slippery, silky sleeve at the door and demanded, "Wait a minute! At least tell me the name of the mental hospital my mother's in! Give me an address, a phone number—something!"

"Oh, Lindsay," Mrs. Mullin said sadly, shaking her head. "Honey. It's in that stack of your dad's mail I brought you the other day. How do you think I found out?"

"Oh," I said numbly, my jaw dropping. "Okay."

I felt a little like Dorothy in *The Wizard of Oz*, finding out that, as desperately as she'd been trying to get home, she'd been wearing the solution on her feet the whole time.

I watched Mrs. Mullin slide into her car and drive away, on her way to church, to some sort of spiritual enlightenment I couldn't even imagine.

"I'm just a baby here," I muttered, feeling more ignorant and uninformed than I'd felt at five and a half, walking onto the set of *Just Me and the Kids* for the very first time. I'd been such an overconfident little kid. And, since then, being able to hear anything anyone said about me had always made me feel like I knew it all.

But now—really, I knew nothing. What was I supposed to do? How was I supposed to decide, when so many factors were unknown? This was like trying to solve an algebra problem full of nothing but variables.

After Mrs. Mullin's car disappeared beyond the edge of my neighbor's leafless forsythia bush, I walked over to the kitchen counter and moved aside the dirty plate from my turkey sub dinner the night before. Under that was a Springdale College employee survey form, an order form for *Trials of a Transcendentalist*, and, at the bottom of the stack, a newsletter from River Valley Institute in River Valley, California.

I wouldn't have glanced at it twice if I'd noticed it three days ago, when Mrs. Mullin originally brought it to me. I would have thought, *How'd Dad get on this mailing list?* and then thrown it away.

But now I pored over the newsletter as if it were a priceless tome containing the wisdom of the ages. I read an article about the purchase of new games for the institute rec room—Clue, Monopoly, Scrabble—like I thought I'd find secret coded messages there about my mother's condition, about what I should do.

The institute didn't sound like a bad place, at least not in its newsletter. It had a rec room and a gym and a "visitation center." None of the articles used the words "crazy," "insane," or "psycho." The patients there were sometimes referred to as "guests." I might have thought River Valley was an up-scale retirement home if it hadn't been for the one column titled "Advocating for the Mentally Ill." And even that was just about writing letters to the California legislators and the U.S. Congress asking for better insurance coverage.

"And that's all it takes?" I said aloud to the sheet of paper in my hand. "You've got someone crazy in your family, you write a few letters, and that's it? You've taken care of your obligation?"

My voice echoed in the empty house. I kept hearing Mrs. Mullin's voice in my head: ". . . it would always be you taking care of her." I thought about what Roz had said Toby did for his mother, intervening to save her from a beating, getting beaten up himself. Almost dying.

"Yeah, but what did my mother ever do for me?" I muttered. "I don't even know her!" I was sixteen years old, I reminded myself. I'd pretty much outgrown the whole needing-a-mother thing. She was nothing to me; I was nothing to her.

But I could still hear her voice too, in my head. *Lindsay. Oh, Lindsay . . .*

I dropped the newsletter on top of my father's other mail.

"Geez, Dad. Why didn't *you* bring Mom here?" I muttered. "You must have known what this house did for me . . . and maybe you."

The frustrating thing about having one parent who's crazy and one parent who's dead was that that left no one to explain. My father had seemed like such a straightforward, dull person when he was alive—why hadn't I discovered at least some of his secrets while he was still around to answer my questions? *Had* he been able to Hear too? *Had* he known what the house had done for me, what it could do for my mother? Or had we just moved here because it was easy, because the house was in my mother's name?

Not that I even knew how my mother had come to own the house, when she'd been in a mental institution for the past sixteen years. Maybe someone had died. I pictured a letter arriving, my father muttering, "Springdale, Illinois? Where's that?" and then him telling some lawyer over the phone, "Yes, all the paperwork should come to me. My wife is . . . ah . . . not in a position right now to handle it herself." And then maybe his contract with the university in California was expiring, things were expensive there and his daughter was falling apart; maybe he applied at Springdale College just by chance, just because we needed a change.

There were too many "maybes" in that line of thinking. I didn't have any clue how things had really happened.

I felt my old resentment boiling up again. Why had my dad died before he told me what I needed to know? Why hadn't he ever told me anything except "Study hard"?

I could just as easily ask, why had my father died at all? Why was my mother in a mental institution? Why was I all alone?

I shoved the whole stack of mail away. It skidded across other letters lying on the counter, letters that had been there the day my father died. On one of the letters—a postcard, actually, urging us to order ink cartridges through the mail—I saw that Dad had scrawled a note to himself. It wasn't *buy milk* or *pick up dry cleaning* like any normal person would write, but *R. Dunder—"live delib." before Thoreau?*

"Oh, Daddy," I whispered, disgust mixing with grief and something like nostalgia. This was just some of my dad's transcendentalist mumbo jumbo. He'd apparently thought that Rutherford Dunder, the insignificant nobody he'd staked his life's work on, had come up with that famous rallying cry of transcendentalism, "Live deliberately," before Henry David Thoreau had thought of it.

As if anybody cared.

Still, I lifted the ink ad out of the sliding stack of mail. When a father leaves behind as little as my father had, anything can become a treasure. A letter offering my dad a better credit card rate slid off the edge of the ink ad, and I saw for the first time that *Thoreau?* wasn't the last part of my father's note. There was a dash, and then a few more words: *Can this help E?*

E? Elaine? My mother?

An electric jolt ran through me, a bolt of intuition. Was it possible that my father hadn't been obsessed with transcendentalism just because he'd been an obscure, dried-up academic? Had his work all along had the broader goal of helping my mom?

Still gripping the ink ad, I whirled around and ran up the stairs. I didn't hesitate at the door of my father's bedroom, like I had before. I shoved the door open and dashed over to his desk. My father's computer sat in the center of the desktop, but I knew anything written on the computer would also be in tidy printouts, lined up in binders across the back of the desk. My dad had been one of those electronically cursed people who could lose data just because of a sneeze, so he always printed out everything. I grabbed one of the binders, and papers surged out the front. I seized one of the papers, and words jumped out at me at random:

"Hearing" references in Emerson . . .

"Ears" references in The Dial . . .

"Listening" references in Dunder's letters . . .

It was all connected. In his own way, my father had been searching for answers all along.

A book slipped out of the binder too, a paperback copy of Thoreau's *Walden*. It fell open to a spot about a third of the way in, as if it had been opened to that page many, many times. I looked down and found the very passage my father's note had referred to:

I went to the woods because I wished to live deliberately, to front only the essential facts of life, and see if I

could not learn what it had to teach, and not, when I came
to die, to discover that I had not lived.

My father had underlined "front only the essential facts
of life" three times and had written in the margin *What E
needs?* He'd underlined that, too.

I read on:

> I did not wish to live what was not life, living is so
> dear; nor did I wish to practice resignation, unless it was
> quite necessary. I wanted to live deep and suck out all the
> marrow of life, to live so sturdily and Spartan-like as to
> put to rout all that was not life, to cut a broad swath and
> shave close, to drive life into a corner, and reduce it to its
> lowest terms, and, if it proved to be mean, why then to
> get the whole and genuine meanness of it, and publish its
> meanness to the world; or if it were sublime, to know it by
> experience, and to be able to give a true account of it in
> my next excursion.

I had tears in my eyes when I stopped, and I told myself
it was only because that Thoreau really was an impressive
writer, even if he might have gotten some ideas from other
people. But it was really because Dad had written, lower
down, in different ink, *For Lindsay, too!*

He'd known. He'd known what I was suffering, and
it wasn't that he hadn't wanted to help. It was that he'd

thought searching old, dusty nineteenth-century texts was the answer.

I began flipping through the book quickly, because surely there was more, surely he'd left other messages for me besides just *For Lindsay, too!* But page after page had underlinings without comment, or faded yellow highlighting that may have just dated back to his college days, long before I was born. Then I remembered how easily the book had fallen open to the first passage. I lay the book down on its spine and let it fall open naturally. This was the underlined passage I came to:

> You may say the wisest thing you can, old man—you who have lived seventy years, not without honor of a kind—I hear an irresistible voice which invites me away from all that. One generation abandons the enterprises of another like stranded vessels.

And beside that, in tiny, cramped lettering, my father had written:

> *I don't hear the voices well enough, and Elaine hears too much. What will Lindsay's fate be? What can I ever tell her? What should I do?*

The tears in my eyes slipped over the edge and began rolling down my cheeks. I touched my father's writing, my fingertips tracing the words that might have been written fifteen years ago or last month—I didn't know. But touching those words, it was like I could feel his despair and desperation, his indecision. This wasn't anything magical or mystical or supernatural. This wasn't my talent kicking in. This was just me understanding my father, for perhaps the first time in my life.

His wife had gone crazy. His daughter had teetered on the brink. He himself had caught only echoes of other people's scorn—I was sure that was what he meant by, "I don't hear the voices well enough." Someone else in a town like Springdale might have asked around for kindred spirits, sought out a support group of sorts. But he was Arthur Scott Curran, awkward and bookish. Dating back to Hicksville Junior College—dating back to high school and before—he'd always been able to rely on his books, sometimes only his books. So that was where he turned for help.

But he also had me. He had me to take care of, and I had no one to rely on but him.

Touching my father's words, I could see dozens of scenes of our lives together.

I saw us sitting at the kitchen table together, silently eating tomato soup and grilled cheese sandwiches. He cleared his throat—he wanted to talk to me. He wanted to tell me about my mother; he wanted to know if the house was enough for me, if it would keep me sane. He wanted to say that he worried about me every time I left the house; he wanted to apologize for letting me be on *Just Me and the Kids*.

But, after he cleared his throat three more times, the only words he could find to say were, "Have you done your homework yet?"

I saw him the night before he died, hovering in the doorway outside my room, pacing in the hall. Every time I glanced up from my computer, he was just stepping into or out of my line of vision. He'd been playing games with himself, thinking, *If she looks straight at me, right in the eye, this will be the night I talk to her. She's old enough to know. . . . But if I say anything about the voices, I'll have to tell her where her mother is. And what if the news about Elaine makes Lindsay think that she's going to go crazy too? What if she does? And how can I talk to her when I haven't found an answer yet? When I know that Lindsay doesn't respect me? . . . Maybe I should wait. Why should I ruin tonight for her? We've got time.*

Our eyes met the next time he passed my room, and all he said was, "How are those SAT practice tests coming?"

I'd been there. I'd heard and seen and known everything he'd said and done. I had no proof of what he'd been thinking, but somehow I was just as sure about that. Maybe it was like religious people having faith—I was so certain that what I believed was true.

"But, really, Dad," I muttered, the tears clogging my throat, just as surely as they streamed down my cheeks. "SAT practice tests? That was all you could talk about?"

I went through the rest of *Walden*, turning each page carefully, hoping for another clue. But there was nothing else about me or my mother, nothing that made me think that my father had been close to finding a solution for any of us. Frustrated, I started to put the book back into the binder, but the flimsy paperback cover slipped off, the ancient glue giving way. And there, on the inside front cover, was another message from my father:

Lindsay will get a better education than I got—she will be able to figure it all out! She'll be able to fix us all!

"Oh, Daddy," I sobbed. "Oh, Daddy!" So I'd misunderstood even this about my father, even his dearest dreams for me. He hadn't wanted me to go to Harvard or Yale so he could brag about his daughter the Ivy Leaguer. He hadn't wanted me to rack up the academic credentials he'd never earned, just for the sake of having them. He'd wanted me to get the best education possible so I could solve our family's problems.

Still sobbing, I reached for the telephone.

Chapter 33

It turns out that it's not that easy to get someone released from a mental hospital, even if you're a Hollywood actress with money and connections. Especially when you call your financial manager on a Sunday, and you've forgotten that you should stop sobbing before you dial his number.

Fortunately, Brendan Crestwell, the man who'd taken care of my financial interests since the early days of *Just Me and the Kids*, had an overinflated sense of his own importance, so his office answering machine included an emergency pager number. And, when I finally reached him, he seemed to take my crying as just a sign that I was a bona fide teen actress.

"Congratulations," he said. "I think this is the very first time that *you've* called me for emergency lawyer money. What did you say you were arrested for—DUI? Drug possession?

Are you at the police station right now? Do you need a reference for a good 'lawyer to the stars'?"

"I wasn't arrested!" I said. "I said I need access to my money to help my mom!"

Crestwell's voice took on a very serious tone, and he began lecturing me about how child stars should never, ever, ever let parents get their hands on their money, because parents really couldn't be trusted, not the way a talented financial manager like Brendan Crestwell could be, because he really did have my best interest at heart, and—

I took a deep breath and interrupted.

"You manage two funds for me," I said coldly. "One is a trust fund that no one can touch until I'm twenty-one. But the other one is my allowance for living expenses, and I can do anything I want with that. Even help my mom, and you can't stop me. Now, did you say you know a good lawyer?"

When I hung up twenty minutes later, I'd hired a lawyer through a conference call and had approved the potential transfer of a large sum of money into his account. Both Brendan Crestwell and the attorney had told me that I was embarking on a ridiculous quest—the attorney had even used the expression, "tilting at windmills," which made me at least feel confident that he'd heard of *Don Quixote*. But I knew they would both do what I wanted them to do. I understood their roles in Hollywood: They had gotten rich by indulging the whims of the famous, and they weren't going to stop now.

Still, I stepped outside as soon as I got off the phone,

just in case. I could hear the attorney dictating instructions into some sort of digital assistant. *Research status of one Elaine Stone Curran, patient at River Valley Institute, River Valley, California, for past sixteen years. . . . Write letter apprising institute of underage daughter's intent to have mother's care transferred. . . . Must check status of daughter's guardian, one Inez Mullin . . .*

I could tell that the attorney would be handing those instructions to his paralegal first thing Monday morning, and even the things that weren't exactly true—like Mrs. Mullin being my legal guardian—would somehow become true, if they needed to be. I could picture the paralegal, a mousy woman who was the real reason the lawyer was so successful, because she was so efficient and smart. I could see what the paralegal was doing right at that moment, bent over her sink dyeing her hair a dull dishwater blond, washing the color out of her life, because a total jerk had hit on her at the grocery store Saturday afternoon, and she didn't want to be the type of woman who attracted that type of man.

I had never been able to see so much before, using my special talents. You might say that I was just imagining it all, but I knew. *I knew.*

I turned my attention to Brendan Crestwell, who was answering the question *Who was that on the phone?* He was sitting back down at the breakfast table, looking with distaste at the slice of cantaloupe on his plate, when what he really wanted was bacon and eggs. The California sunshine streamed in through the wall of windows behind him. His . . . Wife? Girlfriend? . . . *Wife,* I decided . . . went on to ask, *Anything worth selling to the tabloids?*

I stiffened, standing at the edge of my backyard. My leg muscles tensed, a primitive response—as if running away would do any good.

You knew that was possible, I told myself firmly.

In California, Brendan Crestwell toyed with his fork. Normally I would have been able to hear only what he actually said, but somehow now I could sense his thoughts. He'd had an uncle who'd struggled with depression and committed suicide. He remembered the pain, the shame his family had been subjected to, so unfairly, as if his uncle's mental illness had been a stigma upon them all. Even today, Brendan Crestwell had told his wife and children nothing about that uncle.

Brendan Crestwell decisively plunged his fork down through his cantaloupe.

No, he told his wife. *Lindsay Scott is such a has-been. She hasn't been a big name in five years. Nobody's going to be interested in her.*

I sank down into the grass, my legs giving way in relief. It was funny how those words, which could have inflicted such pain, were actually a gift.

Because I knew not just *what* Brendan Crestwell had said, but *why.* I knew he was protecting me.

I ran my hand over the tips of the grass in my yard, then plunged my hand deep, touching the dirt below, separating the blades of grass. This was just what I'd done with my talent, going below the surface of it, down to the roots.

"'Live deep and suck out all the marrow of life,'" I murmured to myself, quoting Thoreau, appreciating him for once.

Then my focus on the scene at Brendan Crestwell's breakfast table vanished, because my brain was suddenly overwhelmed with lots of other chatter.

Oh, I love this episode. . . .

Oh, I hate this episode. . . .

Isn't this the one where Elizabeth gets a pet? . . .

It was only ten thirty. Why was the *Just Me and the Kids* rerun on now?

Oh. Sunday. Right.

Rather than bracing myself against the chatter as usual, fighting it, I let it wash over me. The kid who'd said *I hate this episode* was a thirteen-year-old in Altoona, Pennsylvania, who'd just found out that his parents were getting a divorce. Right at that moment, he hated *everything*.

Oddly, the nine-year-old girl who'd said *I love this episode* was also having a bad day. She had cancer; she was in a hospital in Birmingham, Alabama. She'd been puking her guts out since dawn. As far as she was concerned, the opening notes of the *Just Me and the Kids* music marked the first happy moment of her day.

How could I know all this? How could I avoid caring about those kids, now that I did know?

I heard another voice, a familiar one. It was the prisoner

in Iowa, the one I always heard talking about my reruns. The one who always gave me the creeps.

There you are, he was saying to my image on the TV screen. Somehow I could tell that he had his hand outstretched, that he was stroking the image of my face on the TV.

"No. That's not right," I said aloud, because the prisoner in Iowa had never had TV time on a Sunday morning before. Sunday mornings were supposed to be safe.

I narrowed my focus, listening harder for the prisoner's next words.

My dear little girl, he said, tears streaming down his face.

Somehow I didn't think he would be showing such weakness in prison. I tried to make myself see what was around him. There was a bed with a worn plaid cover. There was faded pea green wallpaper, peeling in spots. There was a plastic brown ice bucket, empty. There were no other inmates. The prisoner was alone.

He wasn't in a prison in Iowa. He was in a hotel room in Illinois, barely a hundred miles away.

Oh, sweetie, the prisoner said, his fingers still tracing the outlines of my face on the TV screen. *I'm out now. I'm coming back to you.*

Chapter 34

Panic seared through me.

I raced back into my house and fumbled for the phone.
I called Roz first.

"Oh, please, come and get me, come and rescue me, tell
Toby and Darnell to come and help too, there's some psycho
coming to get me," I babbled into the voice mail on her cell
phone.

I hung up and tried Mrs. Mullin's number, even though I
knew she wouldn't be home.

"Oh, please. I need help. Please call me as soon as you
get this message. Please, please. I hope you come right home
after church."

And then—it's strange, how now I can't even remember
who called me back first, who assured me most speedily,
"I'm on my way right now." But within an hour I had a yard

full of friends and protectors. Toby and Darnell pushed Mr. Mullin's wheelchair up my sidewalk, lifting it carefully over the uneven spots. Roz brought her mother and stepsister. Mrs. Mullin kept going back and forth to Althea Gooding's house, and reported that Althea had alerted every Hearer in Springdale, and, except for Althea, all of them were standing out in their yards, listening, listening *hard*, just in case they could pick up something helpful, something that might apply to all of us.

And I could see it. Seventy-nine-year-old Rufus Sudlow, over on Virtue Street; twenty-eight-year-old Sarah Grumman, over on Elm; forty-two-year-old Linda Grandee, over on Destiny Trails, telling her five-year-old, *Yes, honey, we are going to stay out in the yard for a long time. Mommy has something important to do out here.*

"There are twenty-two others, aren't there?" I said to Mrs. Mullin when she got back from Althea's.

"What?" Mrs. Mullin said, blinking distractedly at me.

"Besides you and me and Althea, there are twenty-two other Hearers in Springdale, aren't there?" I asked.

Behind her thick glasses, Mrs. Mullin's magnified eyes focused on my face.

"Althea told you that?" she asked.

"No," I said. "I just knew, all of a sudden. I can . . . I can feel them watching out for me."

And I could. I could feel the network we all made, the connections between us, the way they cared about me, even though we'd never met.

Was this part of what my ancestors were looking for when they said they were searching for God? I wondered. Because I cared about my fellow Hearers too. In my mind I could see Linda Grandee's five-year-old reach for an ant that looked like it might be the biting kind, and I gasped, every bit as concerned as Linda herself.

"What happened?" Roz asked, hovering at my elbow. "Is that man—?"

"It's nothing," I said, because I saw the ant dive into its hill. The five-year-old began pulling up dandelion leaves instead. "False alarm."

"Don't you think we should call the police?" Roz asked.

"And tell them what?" Mrs. Mullin asked helplessly, sinking down into a lawn chair that Darnell brought to her. I think he'd borrowed it from a neighbor.

"Well, that this man has threatened Lindsay—which is *true.* We wouldn't have to say how Lindsay knew about the threats," Roz said.

"Police expect evidence," Roz's mom broke in. "Proof."

And I could tell that she was speaking from her own experiences. She hadn't had enough evidence about the man beating up her sister, Toby's mom.

"We'll protect you, Lindsay," Toby said. "Don't worry. We won't let anything happen to you."

And I believed him—sort of. But I could also feel a beat-up brown pick-up truck coming closer and closer and closer. . . .

A cell phone rang—Mrs. Mullin's.

"Yes, yes, you're right. Food would help," she spoke into the phone. "I should have thought of that myself."

She hung up and announced, "Althea Gooding ordered four pizzas for us. They'll be here in fifteen minutes."

And this changed my image of Althea Gooding once again. Who would have thought that she knew how to order pizza?

Within fifteen minutes my front yard had been transformed into a picnic area. Roz and her mother and sister brought out sheets and blankets from my house, and we all spread them out on the ground. Mrs. Mullin called the pizza place and asked for plastic cups and soda pop, along with all the pizzas.

When the pizza arrived, I thought about how, to anyone walking by, our little gathering would look like a party, maybe three generations of family getting together to celebrate a birthday, or just the arrival of spring weather. Or maybe I looked like a Springdale College student entertaining family visiting from out of town as best she could.

But I put down my first slice of pizza half eaten.

"He just drove into Springdale," I announced.

Everyone stopped eating. Darnell stopped talking to Mr. Mullin about how wheelchair athletes always have such impressive arm muscles. Mrs. Mullin stopped talking to Roz's mother about how Springdale College really did offer convenient class schedules for adults who wanted to go back to school. Roz's sister stopped talking to Toby about how much Barkley the dog had grown in the past week.

We all just sat there, waiting.

The brown pickup truck pulled onto my street ten minutes later. The prisoner must have felt our eyes on him. He must have seen how Toby put himself between me and the truck. Maybe he even heard how Toby whispered, "Nobody's going to hurt you."

But the prisoner still got out of his truck. He stumbled out onto the sidewalk, a shrunken old man. Damaged. Broken. Lost. He looked only at me.

"My girl," he whispered, and I heard it both ways, with my ears, and in the same hearing-beyond-hearing way I would have sensed his whisper from the other side of the world.

And that changed everything.

I stood up, brushing past Toby. Nobody stopped me. Nobody said, "No! Wait! What if he has a gun?" Maybe they were seeing everything differently too, now that the prisoner was right there in front of us. Maybe they just trusted me.

I went and stood before the prisoner on the sidewalk. I reached out and touched his wrinkled face.

"Grandpa?" I whispered.

Chapter 35

So what else do you need to know?

Maybe you've figured out how dramatically I'd misinterpreted the prisoner's—my grandfather's—words, right up until that last moment, when I finally really listened. Every time before, when he'd said *I want to hug you. I want to kiss you*, I'd thought he was a child molester. But he was really a lonely father whose life had gone terribly wrong, who'd watched me on TV as a way to remember the happiest moments of his life: the time when his own daughter was a little girl.

It turns out that I have always looked an awful lot like my mother when she was my age. In prison things had gotten a little mixed up in my grandfather's mind. He had almost come to believe that I *was* her, and that his happy past was waiting for him in the house where *he'd* been a little boy.

Which, of course, was my house now.

The network of Hearers in Springdale, who had finally all come out of their houses when they thought I needed them, joined together to help take care of my grandfather. Rufus Sudlow, who'd evidently been a childhood friend, even provided a safe house for him to stay in—because it turned out that my grandfather was a Hearer too. His talents had just developed long after he'd left Springdale. And that's how he'd ended up in prison, when he'd tried to protect himself and his family from someone who was saying awful things about him.

The things my grandfather had heard, the way he'd heard them—that wasn't admissible evidence in court.

And having a father in prison was a factor in my mother's problems. Crazy father, crazy daughter—people expect these things to run in families.

So. Now. It's down to me.

I believe now that I can not just hear what people say about me but also know things about those people that they've never told a living soul. I believe that my gift is actually the gift of extreme compassion, of empathy beyond compare.

Is that something you get when you really, truly search for God? Or am I just crazy?

I cling to Mrs. Mullin's explanation, that the dividing line between sanity and insanity should really be based on what you *do* with what you hear and believe.

And so I go each day to visit my grandfather. He tells

me stories about my mother when she was a little girl, about how she ran and laughed and jumped about, a quick-silver sprite. And then each morning I wake up early and tell those same stories to my mother—me on my balcony here in Springdale, her in her bed at River Valley Institute, in her few moments of lucidity before they give her the next round of drugs. I am trying to reclaim her, to bring her back to herself.

Meanwhile, my expensive attorney and his mousy para-legal have been working magic of their own: Next week my mother is coming to live with me.

I have no illusions about what this will be like. I've arranged around-the-clock nursing care with women I now trust, friends of Roz's mother. And Mrs. Mullin helped me arrange for a psychiatrist to oversee weaning my mother off her medications—a psychiatrist who was born and raised in Springdale, and so must have heard some strange tales about some of its natives; a psychiatrist who also holds degrees in religious studies, and so might be a bit more open-minded about things that cannot be explained by science.

Mrs. Mullin says the psychiatrist would like to help me and my grandfather as well as my mother—a whole family intervention.

But honestly . . . I'm getting where I need to go. I'm well on my way.

Last night Roz and Toby and Darnell and I went over to my grandfather's house. Toby and Darnell delivered a TV for him, along with a complete DVD collection of *Just Me and the Kids.* As we were all setting up the TV, Roz said, "Oh, no, Lindsay. I just thought—this won't make you feel disloyal to your dad, will it, watching TV?"

And I just laughed and said, "That thing about not having a TV in his house—he was kind of misquoted. His point was about frugality and simplifying, transcendentalist stuff. He thought it was stupid to own a TV when you can get just about everything on the Internet." I could have left it at that, but I was with friends. "Now, me, *I* didn't want to watch TV because of the memories. But now . . . now it's okay."

And so Toby popped the DVD in. I hadn't heard the *Just Me and the Kids* theme song in its entirety in five years, but the words were still as familiar as my own face:

Getting by, getting through,
Just me and you . . .
And you and you . . .
Just me and the kids!

At the word "me," Anthony Duzan, who played the father, showed up on the screen. And then with each "you" a new face showed up: Olivia Jerome, my supposed older sister; Dustin Rubino, who played my brother; and last of all, me. My former self beamed out at the world in all her seven-year-old missing-toothed glory. I could understand why every time this show came on in reruns I heard dozens of people talking about the tooth fairy and reminiscing about when they themselves lost baby teeth.

"Ahh," my grandfather said, tears in his eyes. "Your mother lost her two front teeth at the same time too when she was little. She looked just like that."

The show progressed with typical sitcom inanity. The family cat had vanished; the dad was worried that the kids were going to miss the school bus because they were so busy looking for the cat. The bus was due any minute now, but the kids didn't want to leave before they found their cat. . . . Then the camera zoomed in on the smallest girl. She threw her arms out wide and announced, "It's so obvious where Fluffy went!" She was awkward and graceless and practically lisping, because of the missing front teeth.

"Ooh," I groaned from my position sprawled on the floor in front of the TV. "I really was a terrible actress! Everything my enemies said was true!"

"But I loved to watch you," my grandfather said.

"So did I," Toby agreed sheepishly.

I watched the little girl on the screen—who had been me, but wasn't anymore—as she zipped around, solving the mystery of the missing cat. And I could see both viewpoints, that I'd been lovable *and* awful, all at once.

I waited for the pain of knowing how people criticized and mocked me—and how I deserved it!—but it didn't come.

It didn't matter.

I started gasping.

"Are you okay?" Roz asked. "Should we stop the DVD?"

"No, no. It's just—I just realized," I said, bolting upright.

"I would have figured out everything regardless. Even if I'd never begun hearing voices, I would have eventually seen that the people around me were two-faced, and that nobody really thought I was a great actress. It was just that I had that innocence and I wasn't the least bit self-conscious . . . but I would have lost all that no matter what, as I grew up."

"Just about everyone eats from the tree of knowledge eventually," my grandfather said.

Roz and Toby and Darnell were staring at me, as if what I'd said was every bit as incomprehensible as what my grandfather had said.

"You could still *become* a great actress," Toby said after a few moments, which was very generous of him.

"No," I said, shaking my head. "That's okay. I've got other things to do."

And I do.

In the fall I am starting as a student at Springdale College. It's through a special program that lets high school kids take college classes early, so I'm not really under any pressure to have that be my impressive college experience or to begin on any hugely important career path. Thanks to some help behind the scenes from Mrs. Mullin, I was able to design my own studies.

I will be researching obscure branches of transcendentalism, including the one started by Rutherford Dunder, who had a lot of the same ideas as the big guys but who did not feel the need to tell everyone about it. He was opposed to fame, even for good reasons.

But that's not all.

I will also be studying the history of Springdale itself, particularly focusing on the family and descendents of Thaddeus Clay. This study will cover genetics and psychology as well as history, because I have a theory that all the Clay descendents had some interesting traits, even the people that Althea Gooding always assumed were "normal."

I will be joining the college chapter of Habitat for Humanity, which around here means a lot of rehabbing of old houses. I don't know how I'll work it, but somehow I'll manage to get assigned to a house built shortly before the Civil War, and I'll find out all its secrets.

And then I will be planning a trip to Greece and Turkey for next summer, with Mr. and Mrs. Mullin and, if they're well enough by then, my mother and grandfather. I have already begun researching wheelchair accessibility around archaeological digs. If all else fails, I will hire two strong guys—Toby and Darnell, maybe?—who will be able to carry Mr. Mullin's wheelchair, if need be. And if Toby and Darnell go, then of course Roz will want to go as well.

And maybe, on a long trip like that, it will stop being so awkward between me and Toby, with him always mooning over me and me always wanting to say, "Really, you're great. I'm the problem. Don't you see how damaged *I've* been?" Sometimes I think we will end up just being close friends, like he is with Roz. Sometimes I think it will turn out to be more than that. Who knows?

Actually, I don't know how any of this will turn out. But

I have such hope for all my plans and possibilities. I now understand not just the transcendentalists—who wanted to live so fully, to be so aware—but also people such as Walt Whitman, who saw reasons to be awestruck everywhere. I am no longer the girl who made a fool of herself on national TV every single week and didn't even realize it. But I am also no longer the lonely girl who cowered in her safe house, terrified of being noticed.

I am connected now to the Mullins and Althea Gooding and Roz and Toby and Darnell, to all the other Hearers in Springdale, to my mother and grandfather. I am connected to everyone, everywhere. I am connected to God.

And when my "talent" descends upon me now, as soon as I step away from my house, I no longer cringe and cower and brace for pain. I lift my face to the sky and let the revelations wash over me, bringing me truth and insight and purpose. I marvel at all I hear and all I know.

And then that carries me forward, raising me up, urging me on.

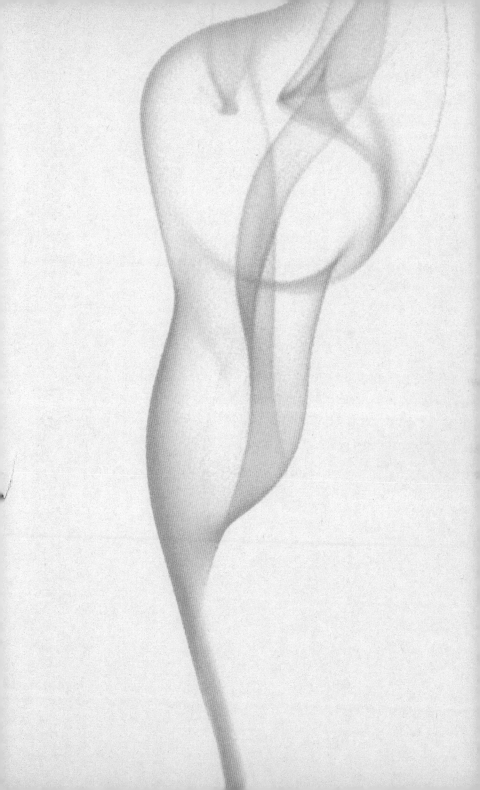

Sometimes *happily ever after* isn't a fairy tale.

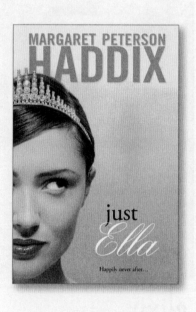

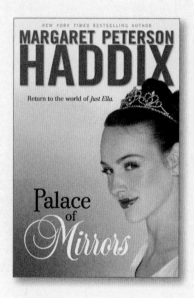

Love is lost but never forgotten . . .

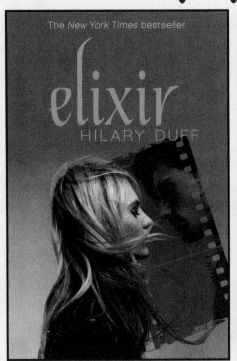

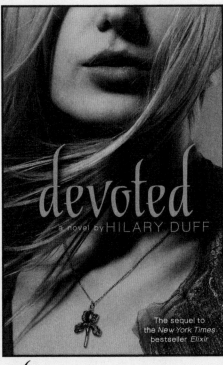

Don't miss the *elixir* series
by New York Times bestselling author
HILARY DUFF

EBOOK EDITIONS ALSO AVAILABLE

A sacred oath,
a fallen angel,
a forbidden love

YOU WON'T BE ABLE TO
KEEP IT *HUSH, HUSH.*